I0656687

Henry Pottinger

Blue and Green

Vol. 2

Henry Pottinger

Blue and Green
Vol. 2

ISBN/EAN: 9783337347284

Printed in Europe, USA, Canada, Australia, Japan

Cover: Foto ©Andreas Hilbeck / pixelio.de

More available books at **www.hansebooks.com**

BLUE AND GREEN

OR,

THE GIFT OF GOD.

A Romance of Old Constantinople.

BY

SIR HENRY POTTINGER.

IN THREE VOLUMES.
VOL. II.

LONDON:
CHAPMAN AND HALL, 193, PICCADILLY.
1879.

(All rights reserved.)

CONTENTS OF VOL. II.

———

BOOK II.—*Continued.*

BOOK III.

BOOK II.

(Continued).

BLUE AND GREEN.

CHAPTER VI.

FIRST LESSONS.

THE exasperation of Constantinople lasted for three days. Furious at the escape of the Emperor, the mob vented their wrath against him in effigy. But the effigy was of flesh and blood; a miserable monk, whose known fidelity to his master procured him the distinction of having his head carried round the city on a spear, followed by a howling multitude, who proclaimed it with scrupulous preciseness, "the head of the friend of the enemy of the Holy Trinity."

The Factions had a glorious time of it, and re-velled in murder, outrage, and incendiarism, which they dispensed with strict impartiality to both orthodox and heretics, being guided in their choice of victims chiefly by the probabilities of booty. But at the expiration of three days a reaction set in. The populace, finding this state of things uncomfortable, and reflecting that in spite of his religious peculiarities there was no one whom on the whole they preferred to Anastasius, insisted upon listening to the Emperor's message, in which, by the voice of a herald, he proclaimed himself willing to acknowledge his errors publicly, to satisfy the Pope, the clergy, the Factions, and the people—in short, everybody—and, if required, to resign his crown; praying only that time might be granted him to recruit his shattered health. Thereupon his friends seized the opportunity, and adroitly turned the popular excitement into a new channel, by representing that unless the most energetic measures were taken to check Vitalian, the Goth was likely to settle the matter after his own fashion, without consulting any one.

Forthwith the city burned with patriotic ardour. Reinforcements and exhortations were despatched to the main army, which was now encamped at the Makron Teikos; the guards condescended to resume their arms and standards, and marched to man the landward fortifications; the catapults, balistas, and other engines on the sea walls were got into the best working order, the vessels of war collected, and the mouth of the Golden Horn closed by a chain extended from the Acropolis to Sycæ.

Intelligence of these formidable preparations

being brought by his spies to the Gothic chief who
was in full march upon the city, he wisely made a
virtue of necessity; halted his army, and sent an
ambassador to declare his satisfaction at the proposed concessions of the Emperor, and to conclude
an armistice until they could be carried out. But
as he intended to see this done, he sent his fleet
round to occupy the Bosphorus, and before long the
great war-ships swept majestically in, and anchored
off Sycæ outside the chain.

Then followed an astounding spectacle, the humiliation of the Emperor, who had slipped quietly
back from his hiding-place in Sycæ.

In all the pomp of Imperial Majesty, Anastasius
passed out from the palace, up the Cochlea or
private staircase which led to the throne of the
Hippodrome, and there the farce of sovereignty
ended and the tragedy of abasement began.

Bending low, amid the triumphant roar of his
rebellious subjects, the monarch humbly removed
his diadem, while the heralds proclaimed his readi-
ness to resign it to any successor whom the populace
might elect. But after the orthodox party had
soothed their outraged feelings by singing the
genuine Trisagion in chorus, and obtaining a
promise that Cæsar's chief instruments in his religious persecutions should be thrown to the lions,
they were good enough to permit him to resume the
emblems of supreme power.

Of this great sight our young Thracian, Belitzar, obstinately refused to become a spectator. When he signified his intention of remaining at home and looking after the boats, the astonishment of his new friends was excessive. Demas swore, Baro chuckled, Antonina opened her dark eyes to their widest, and then tried to laugh him out of it. But when Belitzar had made up his mind to anything there was no shaking his resolution, and so it proved in this case. "By Heaven," said Demas at last, "I like you the better for it, my lad; but I am afraid you will find such high-flown sentiments rather troublesome in the long-run. We hardly understand them here in Constantinople. However, you have plenty of time to get the edge taken off you. Have your own way this time."

And so Belitzar remained quietly by the water for the day, and after the early rush of passengers, all agog for sight-seeing, was over, and before the back rush in the evening began, had leisure enough to listen indignantly as before to the shouts which came out over the wall, and to meditate upon the strange conditions under which an Emperor existed.

But to every other sight and wonder in the great city, the Thracian was duly introduced under the auspices of Demas, and entered into them with the zest natural to his years and rustic simplicity.

He marvelled at the bustle of the teeming Agora, where business and amusement were so strangely

blended ; here a throng of suitors hurrying into the
law courts of the Basilica, there an itinerant juggler
or a troupe of strolling acrobats ; here a knot of
shrewd-looking citizens discussing the state of trade
and the money market, there a gaping circle greedily
devouring the last theatrical advertisements ; here
a band of noisy revellers reeling back from the
night-long festivities of a wedding, there a wretched
criminal being silently hurried off to execution.
He stared with amazement at the treasures of the
shops, at the extravagant equipages and retinues of
the nobles, and the still more extravagant costumes
of their wives and daughters. He laughed at the
grotesque absurdities of the comedies, and sustained
with no greater emotion than strong surprise the
ordeal of the pantomimes. For the mind of Belitzar was guileless and reverential as a child's, and
the complete degradation of woman was a thing he
was at present utterly unable to comprehend.

But he was most taken with the exhibitions of rare
animals and wild beasts in the amphitheatre, at
more than one of which he was fortunate enough
to be present. His hunter's soul waxed enthusiastic
over these. On his return from such a congenial
feast he would open his heart and regale his hosts
with tales of his own forest adventures, his triumphs
over the boar, the wolf, and the stag, and regret
that lions and tigers were not indigenous in Thrace.
Blended with this boyish enthusiasm, there was a

depth and solidity of character, a total absence of
bravado, and yet a grand, simple consciousness of
his own great courage and strength, which won
altogether the heart of the charioteer and caused
even the narrow nature of Baro to expand in something like generous sentiment. The latter, indeed,
occasionally grumbled at what he termed so much
gadding about, and his brother was forced to
remind him that, but for the Thracian, he himself
would never have stirred another step in this
world.

It was a rare treat also to pay a visit with Demas
to the training grounds, and here again Belitzar
was at home, both in theory and practice. He
could ride like a Parthian, and his fresh, unbiassed
judgment on the grand thoroughbreds submitted to
his inspection was highly esteemed by Demas.
The charioteer used to lament bitterly that the
weight and stature of his young friend were a bar
to his acquiring distinction and wealth in the
Hippodrome. "You are too big by far for the
chariot," he would say, despondingly, "and not
nearly come to your full growth either. A thousand
pities! With your cool head and arms of iron you
might take the horses of Achilles himself seven
times round the Spina, and never a graze, I'll be
sworn. It's a glorious trade, though some of the
strait-laced ones pretend to despise it—ay, and a
profitable one, too. When it comes to the point

you may see old Demas put down the gold pieces
with the best of them."

To Antonina the young Thracian was an inexhaustible source of amusement. The city-bred
girl, a coquette from her cradle, and from her position as the daughter of the famous charioteer early
brought into contact with half the young aristocrats
in the city, who regarded the right of lounging
down to the water's edge to discuss sporting matters
with their oracle as an inestimable privilege—had
never yet come across such a nature as Belitzar's,
so fresh and yet so formed, so daring and yet so
simple. She was a tolerable judge. In a higher
rank the fair girl would have been more or less
secluded from all male society until her marriage,
whereas in her present condition she combined the
freedom of the lower classes with a taste for luxury
and elegance belonging to the upper. In the palmy
days of the Hippodrome, the pilots of the winning
teams reaped a far richer harvest than even the
equestrian stars of our own time, and Demas, at
the top of his profession, was able to indulge his
only child with everything in reason, and a good
deal out of it. But Antonina was far too sensible to
aim at being a fine lady. She was content to have
every comfort and many luxuries; to dress well in
accordance with her station, and to be independent;
to go to Theatre, Circus, or Venations, just as she
pleased; to be above vulgarity and below fashion.

The profession of her father was nominally among the most degrading. The Church placed the charioteer in the same category as the actor. But practically the difference between the two was immense. The former could attain eminence only by the display of many excellent and manly qualities; courage, strength, and skill, independence and self-assertion, temperance and incorruptibility. Even Constantinople regarded with suspicion a man who habitually affected the company of actors, but intimacy with a leading charioteer was quite compatible with the highest character and position.

In one direction Antonina was daringly ambitious. She aspired, not without hope, to a marriage into the upper circles; she knew that this aspiration was tacitly approved by her father, and that in case of success, a dowry would be forthcoming which many a fair aristocrat might lack. Moreover, the large hoards of her uncle Baro would certainly be hers one day. But although, for the sake of my high-souled, simple-minded hero, I am anxious to spare as much as possible the reputation of Antonina, it cannot be concealed that her matrimonial projects did not deter her from flirting a good deal in the mean time whenever she got the chance; and the hint of Chrysomalla that she could tell some queer stories about her, was probably as true as the remark that she would never be caught making a fool of herself.

To this charming but dangerous young woman
the companionship of the noble Thracian boy
afforded the greatest gratification. To begin with,
he was particularly handsome; next, he was well
bred—according to his own account descended
from a line of barbarian princes; thirdly, he was
well educated, and had, thanks to his father, the
manners of a gentleman. In his plain working
dress he looked vastly superior to two-thirds of the
fops and coxcombs who came to swagger and simper
and give themselves airs about the place. Then
she wondered at his bravery, his magnificent frame
—it was hard to say which was greater, his strength
or his activity,—his earnestness and presence of
mind, all beyond his years, and above all, at his
innocence. The latter was one of his greatest
attractions. It was such a rare thing in Constantinople, either in man or woman, boy or girl.

For his part Belitzar was equally pleased with
Antonina. His practical acquaintance with the
other sex was limited. For the first time in his
life he found himself in almost daily intimacy with
something superior to a dairy-maid, or buxom
country wench. He had profited too well by his
father's experience to be mistaken as to Antonina's
real social position, or as to the special merits of
genuine ladies; but she was so fresh and fair, so
dainty in her habits and manners, so affable and
winning, that the young rustic may be pardoned if

he in his turn thought the plebeian girl lost nothing by comparison with the over-dressed specimens of female aristocracy whom he had seen lolling in their coaches and barges, or displaying their painted charms in the balconies of the theatres and the galleries of the churches.

Antonina was quite willing that he should fall in love with her; she was used to that kind of thing. But for the present he did not manifest the least intention of doing so. He enjoyed her society with the frank demonstrativeness of a pure young heart yearning for friendship. The year or so by which she was his elder counterbalanced his precocity, and even gave her the advantage over him. He told her everything, and consulted her on every point. He confided to her all the details of his short life, and his hopes and longings for the future, and he asked little or nothing in return. It was most agreeable to her to be squired by a youth of such very presentable exterior, whose whole soul lay open to her, so that she could turn him to the best account, and against whom she had little need to be on her guard. His unsuspicious eyes were not likely to penetrate her fair mask and detect the subtlety and falseness of her inner nature.

And so the days slipped away; and after the novelty of sight-seeing had in some degree worn off, Belitzar, who found himself strangely contented with his present lot, buckled strenuously to the business of the ferry and boat-yard, and saw but little of Antonina until the evening. Then he would stroll to the charioteer's house, and more than once found Antonina in converse with the stolid-looking young officer, Paris, who had been so conspicuous on the night of the Emperor's escape. This fact alone was sufficient to secure for the guardsman the respect and gratitude of Belitzar, and to him it seemed but natural that those who had been associated on so important an occasion should continue their intimacy, especially as the visits of the young sprigs of fashion to the charioteer's house were by no means unfrequent. At first Paris eyed the intruder superciliously, and was inclined to stand upon his dignity, but at the instigation of Antonina he unbent to the extent of declaring that the Thracian was a splendid young fellow, and would look well in a cavalry uniform. After which concession the two became friendly, as far as the difference of station permitted.

There were evenings, moreover, when the young people were allowed to take boat on their own account, and spend the cool hours after sunset happily enough among the throng of pleasure craft which beset the mouth of the harbour; and as Antonina could generally get her own way with either her father or her uncle, an afternoon row round the Gothic fleet, or even a trip to Chalcedon, where Demas had some relations, was now and then accomplished.

With all this Belitzar could not escape occasional fits of despondency. The dependence of his position galled him, and his spirit longed for the freedom of his Thracian home, the green glades of the forest, and the unpeopled slopes of the Balkan. While this heaviness of heart was upon him he was glad to slip away in his hours of leisure, and betake himself to some quiet spot where he could indulge his melancholy reflections without interruption. The words of his dying father haunted him : " There are great things in store for thee, my son." Were they but the final suggestion of paternal love and pride, or, as some wise men believed, did the approach of death indeed endow the spirit with prophetic vision ? When should he be cheered by the glimpse of a nobler destiny ? He thought over the events which had taken place since his father's death, and, being piously brought up, tried hard, poor boy, to discern in them the finger of Providence. His casual meeting with Baro, their capture by the Bulgarians, and the consequent loss of his small store, which left him utterly without resources—that would in all probability have occurred had he continued his journey alone ; moreover, he would certainly have resisted, and as certainly have lost his life. Then that young officer—such a contrast to his men ; so gallant, high-bred, and pleasant-voiced. At this distance of time, when the bitterness had passed

away, he could not help liking him; he believed
that, in spite of his reckless, bantering tone, he had
been really sorry for him. Would they ever meet
again? he wondered. Ah! there was one more
unfortunate than himself; ruined, cast out by his
relations, driven by sheer despair into the service of
a rebel, into taking arms against his Emperor; his
lady-love false to him, and now doubly false—to
herself. Belitzar had learnt from Antonina the particulars of the nine days' wonder which had amused
the gossips of the city, but in his modesty he never
spoke of the guilty whisper which he had over-
heard as the young bride of Malchus parted from
her apish adorer at the water-side. Were there
many like her? His father was wont to be silent
on such matters, but he had hinted more than once
at the depravity of Byzantine society. Were the
upper classes worse than the lower? Antonina
—could she ever behave like that?

At this delicate point we will leave the young
Thracian to his musings.

In the mean time the man upon whom he was
wasting his pity, in the best of health and in
tolerable spirits, was clattering and jingling, with a
score of lances at his heels, along the northern
road, the bearer of an order for the release of
Hypatius, who ever since his capture at the
commencement of the war had been consuming his
very heart in vexation and weariness, as he paced

the narrow bounds of the gloomy Cimmerian fortress to which he had been consigned, and looked out hopelessly over the dreary expanse of the Euxine Sea.

At the declaration of the truce, Sittas, much to his disgust, had been recalled to head-quarters, and forced to kill time as best he might in the camp of Vitalian.

One morning, when he was feebly enjoying with a comrade a pitcher of indifferent wine, and a cast of the dice for low stakes, a great stir in camp interrupted the pair at their mild recreation, and it was presently reported that the Patrician Secundianus, brother-in-law of the Emperor and father of Hypatius, had come to implore the pity of Vitalian, and if possible to ransom his son.

Since his departure from the capital, but little news of a private nature had reached Sittas, and therefore he resolved not to lose the present opportunity of making up arrears. It so happened that the first person he encountered in the suite of Secundianus was a young gentleman, the nephew of the Prefect Proclus, with whom he had been intimate in society, and who had served during the campaign in the Imperial army. By dint of much questioning—for Eulalius was loth to hurt the feelings of his exiled friend—Sittas at last elicited the whole truth, and learnt the perfidy of his intended. The wound to his vanity—I dare not say to his heart—was severe; but it was to a certain extent mitigated by the subsequent remarks of his informant, who ventured to congratulate him on his escape, inasmuch as the heartless mercenary jade was making his uncle's life a burden to him, and carrying on disgracefully with some one else. He even went so far as to hint that it might cause a reaction in Sittas' favour, and advised him not to make a fool of himself and get killed before his luck turned.

And Sittas, although he swore a bitter oath never to trust man or woman again, and grew more reckless and case-hardened than ever, plucked up heart, and with an eye to the future which did him credit, volunteered to be the bearer of Vitalian's order, trusting that if he should ever stand in need of a friend at court, he might not be altogether forgotten by Hypatius.

CHAPTER VIII.

PORPHYRIO.

The summer was far advanced, and still the truce continued ; the arrival of the Papal Legates was daily looked for, and there were many who were sanguine enough to believe that on this occasion the Emperor would sacrifice his own opinions to the welfare of his people, and make such concessions as to leave no excuse for further hostilities on the part of Vitalian. In the mean time the city was unusually tranquil. But on the morning which this chapter commemorates there was excitement among the inhabitants of the villas, suburban and marine ; for the boats which brought in the early supply of fish had also brought the intelligence that Porphyrio was disporting himself in the Propontis, and slowly progressing towards the capital, and that the distinguished stranger might be expected in the course of a few hours.

Now Porphyrio was a phenomenon, an anomaly,

a monster! neither more nor less than a gigantic whale! Under what stress of circumstances or through what peculiarity of disposition the huge cetacean had exchanged the cold expanse of the northern brine for the confined and tepid waters of the south; whether, Columbus-like, impelled by a spirit of exploration, or whether seeking a lasting refuge from the persecution of the Hyperborean mariner, he had become entangled in the labyrinths of the Mediterranean, it is difficult to say; but the indisputable fact remains, attested by the chronicles of the time, that, for a long series of years, Porphyrio—for so the Byzantines had christened him —did haunt the vicinity of the Archipelago, at intervals passing through the Hellespont, and working up to disport himself beneath the very walls of the capital, and even on rare occasions penetrating to the waters of the Euxine, where he eventually met his fate, and was stranded at the mouth of the river Sangaris.

Nor did the strength and spirits of the mighty barbarian appear to be at all affected by the comparative mildness of his adopted climate. There was no relaxation about Porphyrio, and his unwieldy gambols at times caused infinite discomfiture and consternation among the fishing boats and pleasure barges which crowded the straits.

It is true that, if extensive in area, the excitement was mild in degree, for neither the weather nor the scene were conducive to the indulgence of violent emotions.

The sapphire water glittered in the morning sun glassy and unruffled, save where a transient patch of tiny wavelets came and passed upon the surface like breath upon polished steel, showing where some zephyr was attempting to be energetic and failing signally. The vast outlines of the gleaming city and the wooded slopes of the Asiatic shore were wrapped in a delicate haze prophetic of noontide heat, the sombre fringe of tall cypresses stood out blackly defined against a cloudless sky, and the far snows of Olympus hung like a white vapour on the horizon.

Had the good ship Argo herself come sailing by, with the golden fleece conspicuous in the rigging, or the Cyanean rocks resumed their floating propensities and dropped down to anchor opposite the Golden Horn, it was not to be thought of that any one should much disturb himself on such a morning.

Perhaps the most languid phase of interest might have been found in a group of men, whom the rumour had tempted to quit the cool, luxurious chambers of the Villa Ecebolus, to lounge through the hot garden and to subside in the shade of a portico of snowy Proconnesian marble built out over the deep clear water. From this a flight of steps led down to a landing place, where three or four

gaily-painted and gilded barges were reflected line
for line in the liquid mirror; the swarthy crews, a
medley of brown legs and arms and white linen,
lying asleep beneath the awnings or basking motionless in the sun. In the centre of the portico spouted
a fountain, crowned by a statuette of Venus Ana-
dyomene, and in the lower basin of this stood cooling
a tall vase of Chian wine, and another filled with
a kind of sherbet of amber tint and delicate
perfume.

Of the four men assembled, two, recumbent in a
cushioned recess of the portico, were enjoying a
siesta, while a boy attendant, provided with a long-
handled ostrich fan, gently agitated the air above
the sleepers and kept off the flies. The other pair,
lying side by side on silken litters, with their heads
and arms projecting over the balustrade, were
engaged in fishing, if, indeed, that could be called
fishing which consisted in dangling a hook in the
water until a turn of the wrist had secured a victim,
when the line was handed to an attendant to haul
up and rebait. There was no lack of sport, for
through the pellucid water scores of many-hued
fishes could be seen fighting for the lure as it
descended, and a large basket at hand was half
filled already with the glittering spoil.

Another page devoted himself to the care and
distribution of the contents of the vases, and a
fifth, perched beside a statue on the huge block of

marble which terminated the balustrade, was keeping a sharp look-out for signs of Porphyrio.

"I believe," said Ecebolus, who was himself one of the anglers, watching with feeble interest the struggles of a fine mullet which was being carefully drawn up the face of the stonework, "I believe this story about Porphyrio to be a myth; or else he has changed his mind and turned back. Shall we send for the slaves, my Eulalius, and be carried to the house? It is too hot to walk."

"Now we are here," replied his companion, of whom we have already heard in the Cynegium and the suite of Secundianus, "we may as well stay a little longer. I like catching these fellows, and the sound of the fountain is delicious. Besides, it would be a shame to disturb those two. How the military secretary is enjoying his holiday! And Paris is smiling sweetly in his sleep, like an infant."

"Dreaming of Antonina, possibly," said Ecebolus, in a low tone. "How will that end, think you? You know him better than I do. Will he be ass enough to marry the girl?"

"Nothing more likely. He has a ponderous affection for her, and is a youth of high moral principle; not at all like us. Well, she will have money. Demas is as rich as a Jew, they say; and Paris has little beyond his good blood and his pay. He might do worse."

" Worse! A charioteer's daughter! And I
hear you say this—a man who boasts his descent
from the old Flavians! Moreover—— " but hero
Ecebolus checked himself.

" Exactly. Let us be discreet. The connection is
not aristocratic, I allow; at the same time he has
only himself to please. The girl will play the fine
lady well enough if she gets the chance, and in my
opinion she will. I will have a bet with you. Look
at that big fellow with the long snout; I catch him
against you for ten solidi. I will take your fifty
about the double event, if you like, that I hook the
fish and the girl the guardsman. He is shy——
Keep that parasol out of sight, boy. By Jupiter! I
have him. Now be careful. You young bungler,
you've lost him! "

" How keen you are! " sighed Ecebolus. " If it
is any satisfaction to you, stick the hook into
Calliparæus and pitch him into the water."

" It is too much trouble; I'll let him off this
time. Ah! my friend, to appreciate this sort of
thing you ought to have been through a campaign.''

" I can believe that. It must be almost worth
while enduring the discomfort and fatigue for the
sake of the fresh impulse it gives to a man's life.
Look at us poor jaded, bored stay-at-homes; moving
heaven and earth to find a new sensation to goad
our callous senses; moaning over the utter stale-
ness of existence; and you, you return to plunge

into it with all the eagerness of a schoolboy into
a pastry-cook's."

"The worst is it won't last. I dare say I shall
soon be sick of everything again. I have already
lost the magnificent appetite I brought home with
me. But suppose you try the same physic. The
war is sure to break out afresh; why not turn
soldier? You are certain of a commission; they
want men of your stamp. If we are not sent to
the front again I'll keep house for you, until you
come back, upon the most economical scale."

"Men of my stamp, indeed! How you misjudge
me! My dear Eulalius, I have positively no
energy, and I hate fighting. I should desert on the
first opportunity. One of these days, perhaps, I
may try to buy a peaceful governorship and retire
into provincial respectability."

"You choose to talk like that, but we know
better. You see one can't forget how you behaved
in that affair at the Cynegium long ago, and on
more than one occasion since."

"Pshaw! mere excitability. But have your
own way; it is too hot to dispute. I wish this
cursed fish would make his appearance, or send
word that he doesn't mean coming."

"By the way, Ecebolus, I hear you made a
voyage this summer."

"Yes, I have not long returned from Tyre."

"I trust you found that most amiable of old

gentlemen, your father, in perfect health and
prosperity."

"Eminently prosperous, but not so well as I
could have wished."

"Ah! the best of us are but mortal. The
prosperity is a great point, though. And as open-
handed as ever?"

"Indeed, yes. The dear old man's generosity
overwhelmed me. I own to certain exorbitant
requisitions, but he never so much as murmured."

"What a glorious example to all parents! Not
that I wonder at it. It would take a heart of stone
in either man or woman to refuse you anything, my
dear Adonis."

"There, you are flattering me again; it is lucky
that I am naturally modest. And so you saw poor
Sittas? How was he looking?"

"Grandly; in the rudest health, and bronzed as
an Arab. He is a good deal altered in some ways.
There is a harshness and swagger about him which
I never noticed in old times. I expect those
Bulgarians try a man a good deal."

"I should think so. I hear that they stink
horribly, and swarm with vermin."

"They are splendid light horsemen for all that,
and never waste an arrow. It says a good deal
for Sittas that he can manage them; as a rule
they will follow none but their own people."

"Ah! but he had a talisman of some sort; his

great-grandmother's gold collar, I think it was, and used to claim cousinship with Vitalian."

"I wish to Heaven he was on our side. Not that I care a great deal about the religious question. Altogether I am inclined to think the Goth is in the right. But it would be so awkward if one chanced to meet him in the field."

"Scarcely more so than belonging to different Factions in the city. In such a case we are not forced to cut each others' throats, if we don't wish to. What's this, I wonder?"

Here a slave entered the portico with a letter, which he delivered to the Tyrian.

"The devil!" exclaimed Ecebolus, after reading it; so loudly that Paris woke with a start, and John of Cappadocia roused himself deliberately to listen.

"Wait outside," said the Tyrian to the slave. "Now, my friends, what do you suppose this is?"

"Can't she come?" asked John, yawning.

"From Demas," guessed Eulalius. "Something amiss with the horses."

"Bill," hazarded Paris, laconically, but with great feeling, though he was only half awake.

"You are all wrong, gentlemen," said Ecebolus. "I am threatened with a visit from his Highness the Prince of Prigs, Justinian. He proposes, if I am at home, to follow his messenger shortly. What do you think of that?"

"Is it the first time you have been so honoured?" inquired Eulalius.

" The very first. Our acquaintance hitherto has
not gone beyond formal civilities, and the discussion of the usual topics, the weather, the war,
and the rest of it. And now he chooses the heat of
the day to pay me a visit. Can one so wise care
about a trifling whale ? "

" He never does anything like other people," said
Eulalius. " Had we not better conceal the wine ?"

" Or at least hang something over that fresco ? "
suggested the Cappadocian, pointing to a glowing
illustration of the loves of Mars and Venus.

" He must take us as he finds us," said Ecebolus.
" Calliparæus, write that I lay myself and my house
at the disposal of the noble Justinian."

And in truth there was no reasonable ground for
these sneers; for when the nephew of Justin did
make his appearance, nothing could be more con-
ciliating or affable than his manner.

" This intrusion into your paradise is a pleasure
I have long anticipated," he said, gracefully
saluting Ecebolus; " and no one but a hermit like
myself would have deferred it until now. I beg
of you to make allowance for my constitutional
reserve."

" The compliment to my poor house is the
greater," replied Ecebolus, " that your visit is the
happy result of mature resolve, and not of the
hasty caprice which governs most men."

And after the interchange of these pretty speeches

the party fell to discussing the probability of
Porphyrio putting in an appearance, and other
more commonplace subjects.

It would probably have been difficult for Justinian
to have analyzed to his own satisfaction his reasons
for seeking a closer acquaintance with Ecebolus.
The wealth and luxury of the young Tyrian, which
attracted most people, had certainly little to do
with it, and the personal fascination which he
exercised over all who came in contact with him
was to a great extent lost upon his cautious and
unsympathetic visitor. A stronger motive, but one
only intelligible in connection with Justinian's
marked idiosyncrasy, might arise from the self-
accusation of having conceived an unreasonable
dislike to Ecebolus at the moment when he was
displaying the nobler side of his nature, and even
in consequence of such display; in this charitable
light, the visit might be regarded as a species of
mild atonement or self-mortification. It might
have been prompted by curiosity to learn more of a
character which combined such opposite attributes
—the external effeminacy and studied selfishness
of an habitual sybarite, with a generosity, self-
sacrifice, and contempt of danger not unworthy of
heroic days. If so, was there a lurking hope that
the former might be found to predominate so largely
as to render the latter dwarfed and insignificant by
contrast? When people have trained themselves

with much labour to a formal standard of excellence,
it is annoying to find a graceless, ungrafted sinner
throwing out spontaneous shoots of virtue, when by
rights the fruit ought to be uniformly evil. The
thorn has no right to grapes, or the thistle to figs.

But for the very pith and marrow of the
incentive I think we must go yet deeper into the
recesses of Justinian's heart. A faint vision of a
pale young face, with eyes almost too large, and a
wealth of chestnut hair encircled by a simple white
wreath; a vision which, day by day, month by
month, in spite of study and seclusion, of fast and
prayer, grew more and more distinct; a restless
desire to learn more about the incarnation of that
vision; a thought which, like a hissing viper,
would creep up and fasten upon him, 'There is one
who can tell you all, more than you might like to
know: if you, the student, the ascetic, cannot forget
her, do you imagine that he, the libertine, has
neglected his opportunity?'—shall we not find
among these the true motive of Justinian's visit?

* * * * * *

"I must not omit to congratulate you, sir," said
Justinian, turning to Eulalius, "on the approaching marriage of your fair cousin, while I rejoice to
think that Count Hypatius will be able to forget
his melancholy captivity in these new and enviable
fetters."

"Indeed, he requires some consolation," said

Eulalius. "The trial has been most bitter, and the effects are not likely to wear off for a long time to come. His health has suffered severely, and, strange as it may appear, he looks forward to nothing so much as complete retirement and repose."

"At the first glance one would imagine he must have had enough of both," said the Cappadocian. "It is true, then, that his Highness intends to relinquish public life altogether, as far as his station will permit, and to take no part in affairs military or political?"

"With Cæsar's consent he proposes to adopt such a course for some time at least. In the mean time his duties at Court will devolve upon his brother Pompey."

"The state must lament the loss of his valuable services," said Justinian, in his grave, deep tones, while the quick-eyed Cappadocian noted the sarcastic gleam which accompanied the words, "and console itself by the hope that its future ruler may recover a healthy tone of mind and body. We can scarcely wonder at his resolution. I can easily understand that no amount of excitement or exertion could prostrate a man so utterly as the pining and chafing in solitary captivity, and such a captivity as the Count has undergone, so desolate and cheerless, so remote from every sphere of civilized action, such a hopeless severance from all that was near and dear to him."

"Encompassed by unintelligible sheep-skinned savages," said Ecebolus, taking up the theme, "obliged to eat the flesh of horses and to drink the milk of mares, and exposed to the hospitable importunities of the female barbarian—also sheep-skinned. Faugh! The fair sex are notoriously attentive to prisoners, especially during the temporary absence of the male population. Am I not right, sir?"—he had the audacity to appeal to Justinian. "Did you not find the ladies of Ravenna lay themselves out to alleviate the sorrows of the exile?"

Justinian laughed good-humouredly. "I am but a poor judge," he said; "if there were any so charitable I fear they found me sadly unresponsive. But there were few sorrows in my case; a hostage in the Court of Theodoric is a very different thing to a prisoner at Acres Castellum."

"By Saint Venus! I pity the Count from the bottom of my heart. However, his troubles are over. I hear that the preparations for the wedding are on a splendid scale, and that a special theatrical entertainment is to be provided for the Factions, at the expense of the noble bridegroom. Is it true?"

"Quite true," replied Eulalius. "We shall all be bidden in due time, and I happen to know that the bill of fare will be of the choicest. Chrysomalla hinted at a performance which was to rival or eclipse her celebrated Leda; if she allow that, you can fancy it must be something out of the way."

" You know Chrysomalla ? " asked Ecebolus.

" Slightly, my friend. You see, I have been recently employed—as a relation of the bride—in making occasional calls at the theatre—on matters of pure business."

" Of course we all go there on business," said Ecebolus, " when we are not merely spectators. Tell us more. I am quite behind the times since my journey to Tyre."

" Now I come to think of it," said Eulalius, " you deserve a public testimonial. Chrysomalla's pearl of price is one of the girls for whom you did champion at the Cynegium ! "

" You don't say so ! I congratulate her—both, in fact. It must be the beauty, of course. I remember her. She had the most magnificent eyes, and reddish hair. I made some inquiries about her and her sisters at the time, and learnt that they were intended for the stage; but I had nearly forgotten the affair altogether."

" Is it possible ? And yet you kissed her ! "

There was a moment of silent astonishment, for the speaker was Justinian. His round eyes were fixed on the Tyrian with an unaccountable look of wonder and satisfaction. Ecebolus stared, and Justinian began to appear slightly uncomfortable.

"Now you mention it," exclaimed the Tyrian, with a gay laugh, "I believe I did, in a paternal sort of way. So you were there, and saw me! I am grateful to you for recalling the fact. One can't be expected to recollect everybody one kisses. But what has been done once may be done again."

"Scarcely so paternally, perhaps," suggested the Cappodocian; but for some reason he glanced keenly at Justinian as he spoke, and for the second time the latter betrayed faint but undoubted signs of confusion and annoyance, even to the extent of a slight change of colour. "It is rather curious," resumed John, "but I too was interested in those girls. Their father, Acacius, was an old client of mine. He sent for me on his death-bed and made me swear to assist his daughters in their appeal to the Factions. I did so, much against my better judgment. Theodora, whom you speak of, is a very singular girl."

"She is singularly beautiful," exclaimed Justinian, earnestly, "and her behaviour during that scene at the Cynegium was superb. I shall never forget it—never!"

With some difficulty John repressed an ejaculation at this unwonted enthusiasm. A ray of light flashed across his speculative intelligence, and he was tempted to cry, like the Greek of old, "Eureka, Eureka!"

"And she has become an actress," continued

Justinian, meditatively. "Her rare young life is
to be wasted in making a public exhibition of herself!—an indecent one, most probably."

"Most certainly," said Eccbolus, with bland correction. "But, my dear sir, why use the term
wasted? Has the Byzantine public no appreciation?
Her early success argues a glorious future. Of
course she has appeared already; Chrysomalla is
too wise a woman to produce an utter novice on so
important an occasion, however lovely she may be."

"She has, in fact, been on the boards for the
last few weeks," said Eulalius, "but purposely kept
in the background, you understand; playing minor
comic parts to her sister Comito's lead, who is also
a charming girl with considerable talent. But Theodora has real genius, and is equal to anything—so
Chrysomalla declares. She has spared no pains
on her education."

"Amiable woman!" said Eccbolus. "Well, I
hope we shall not all quarrel about this girl; we all
seem to take a great interest in her, and between
us can throw a good deal of light on the subject.
All but Paris. Paris, can you not contribute a
single scrap of information to the general fund?"

"I know of a boy whose twin brother is Chrysomalla's page, if that is any good to you?" said
the guardsman, indolently.

"Not much; but the fact is interesting. Chrysomalla's page! What an opening for ingenuous

youth! I suppose the authorities wink at the excess in consideration of her long and meritorious services. They don't let actresses keep pages as a rule. There was a younger sister, I remember, a mere child; does anybody know what has become of her?"

"There I can help you again," said Eulalius. "She was carefully baptized and taken into my cousin's household; lately she has been transferred, by particular desire, to that of Juliana Patricia."

"A lamb of a very different fold. She will, no doubt, develop into a young saint, and be in danger of canonization one of these days; while her sister's shame is to be the crowning glory of Count Hypatius' wedding. H'm! Virgines ad Lenones. Well, it is a queer world. I suppose, one way and another, we all fulfil the end for which we came into it."

"Μη φυναι νικᾱ,"* said Justinian, rather dismally; and, as no one seemed disposed to contradict him, there was a pause in the conversation.

"Porphyrio! Porphyrio!" screamed the boy perched beside the statue. "Here he comes!" and in a minute the whole party were on their legs, craning over the balustrade and twisting their necks after the uncomfortable fashion of spectators on a racecourse, and people generally who are desirous of seeing round a corner.

---

* Not to have been born, were best.

As Ecebolus presently remarked, when the great fish had reached a point nearly opposite the portico, " there was not much to see, after all."

Midway between the mouth of the Golden Horn and Chrysopolis the sunny blue of the current was streaked with a darker, broken line like the wake of a ship, and flecked with white foam. At intervals a huge, gleaming black mass rose above the water, spouted forth a column of glittering spray, and weltering for an instant on the surface, sank again to reappear further up the channel; for Porphyrio, probably in search of cooler waters, was evidently bent on an excursion to the Euxine. A whole fleet of small boats hovered along either shore, prudently keeping out of the track of the monster.

" ' Quanto delphino balæna Britannica major,' " quoted Justinian.

" Very disappointing," said Ecebolus. " Now, if the authorities had a little of the spirit of their forefathers, they would catch Porphyrio alive some-how, flood the amphitheatre, and exhibit him. What a triumph of spectacle ! Galba's funambulist elephants would be a joke to it. There is no enter-prise nowadays. But what are those boats about ?"

Porphyrio by this time had passed the mouth of the harbour, and was nearing the station of the Gothic fleet, while the troubled water in his wake began to be dotted by numerous craft, which, now that the danger had passed, pushed boldly out into midstream.

As Ecebolus spoke two large galleys were seen at
a considerable distance advancing side by side, and
from the rapid rise and fall of their long banks of
oars, evidently bearing down at a great pace to
meet the leviathan.

"Is it possible they mean to attack Porphyrio?"
exclaimed Justinian.

"By Heaven, they do!" cried Ecebolus, positively excited, as he sprang nimbly on to the
balustrade, and held on by the waist of a placid
marble Nereid. "The barbarians are going to show
us some sport. I can see figures standing in the
bows."

The distance was too great to make out exactly
what happened, but the result was soon evident.
As Porphyrio rose to the surface and spouted, one
of the galleys boldly drew close to him; there was a
flash of steel, a shout, a clamour of many voices, a
sound of grinding and crackling timber, and a cloud
of sparkling foam. When it subsided, the daring
galley was seen slowly gyrating in a miniature
whirlpool, most of her crew apparently turning
somersaults over the thwarts, and the water strewn
with the shivered fragments of a whole bank of oars
which Porphyrio had demolished in his angry
plunge.

"Well done, Porphyrio!" shouted Ecebolus, in
high glee; "there is a lesson for those swaggering
barbarians. The galley is sinking;" and surely

enough they could see the crew scrambling out of her on board of their consort, which had ranged alongside.

But the vengeance of Porphyrio for his inhospitable reception was not yet complete. As he dived, the whale headed back down the channel, running in towards the European shore, and all at once his huge bulk surged up directly in front of the portico where our friends were assembled, and in the very midst of the flotilla of boats. One thrash of his mighty tail, and the nearest, a large wherry, was spun into the air like a nutshell, and then Porphyrio went rollicking back into the Propontis, leaving as reminders of his presence a wherry floating bottom upwards, three persons struggling in the water, and a great wave which set the barges at the portico steps rocking and bumping, and lapped angrily against the marble.

This terrible example caused such a panic among the surrounding boats, that, plying their oars with might and main, they dispersed in every direction, leaving the late occupants of the wherry to save themselves as best they might.

The unfortunates consisted of a man, a girl, and a boy. The first had been pitched by the shock to some little distance, and was evidently uninjured and a strong swimmer, for he could be seen bravely breasting the current. The boy, by good luck, splashed into the water close to the capsized boat, which he laid hold of, and by a desperate effort managed to wriggle on to the keel, where he sat astride like Arion on his dolphin, and so avoided black death. But the girl was in imminent peril. Apparently she had been stunned or disabled by the concussion, for almost without a struggle she drifted away from the boat and sank slowly, the last thing visible of her being the gleam of her gay shawl as it gradually melted into the azure crystal of the tide.

" By God, she is lost ! " exclaimed Ecebolus; and in three bounds he had cleared the steps, and alighted with a crash on the bottom boards of the nearest barge.

" Row ! you lazy, gaping idiots ! " he shouted; " row for your lives ! A hundred drachmas to each if we get there in time."

But neither the Tyrian's presence of mind nor the exertions of the slaves could have been of the least avail had it not been for the skill and energy of the swimmer. Three several times he dived without result, but at the fourth attempt an excited cheer from the spectators announced that he had reappeared with the girl in his arms ; and when the barge returned to the villa, it landed our young hero Belitzar, the boy Andreas, and, to the horror of the party and the undisguised grief of Paris, the inanimate body of Antonina, the charioteer's daughter.

CHAPTER VIII.

THE DEBASING OF THE GIFT.

ANTONINA was not quite drowned. Thanks to the
assiduous care of the female portion of the Tyrian's
household, vitality slowly reasserted itself, and
before evening she was sufficiently restored to allow
of her being moved in a litter to her father's roof.
The accident, which might have been so disastrous,
turned out to be a fortunate circumstance for more
than one concerned in it. Paris, rendered unusually demonstrative by the melancholy sight of
Antonina's waxen lids and cold white face, made
no attempt to conceal his affection, or that he regarded her in the light of his future bride; and no
restorative was so efficacious in bringing back the
blood to her cheeks and the light to her eyes, as the
sly allusions of the saucy, chattering, but compassionate maidens who attended her to the
difficulty they had experienced in preventing the
anxious guardsman from forcibly invading the

women's quarter, and to the look of delight and thankful ejaculation with which he received the news of his mistress's return to life.

Of all this Belitzar knew nothing, but as he hurried back with Andreas to relieve the anxiety of Antonina's relations, his heart also was overflowing with happiness. Not only had he the delicious consciousness of having played the man that morning, and saved the life of one whose peril had opened his eyes to the fact that her friendship was the great joy and solace of his existence, but the first ray of hope as to his future had at length dawned upon him. For Justinian, struck by the boy's strength and courage, but especially by the nobility and modesty of his demeanour, had actually offered him a place among his personal attendants, with the near prospect of being enrolled in his uncle Justin's body-guard, if he persisted in his preference for a military career above all others. For a friendless youth such as Belitzar it would be impossible to exaggerate the value of this opening. The household of Justinian was in itself a most honourable sphere of service, but the Domestics of a great officer like Justin were almost invariably picked men, selected either for conspicuous physical qualities or for proved valour. Their pay, accoutrements, and general advantages were greatly superior to those of the ordinary soldier, and they had an especial chance, even on home service—and over this

Belitzar rejoiced with exceeding joy—of manifesting their zeal and fidelity as individuals, and of eventually rising to military command. From such a beginning, indeed, had sprung the splendid position of Justin himself.

Nor was Andreas excluded from the general satisfaction. His wet pockets were full of money, and he had the promise of Paris, who was much gratified by finding the boy sobbing sympathetically in a corner of the women's corridor, that one of these days he should be permanently employed in the service of his benefactress Antonina.

For a brief space after these events Belitzar entered upon one of those transient periods when the sands of life run all golden. The boy was not aware how rapidly his romantic affection for Antonina was ripening into a deeper feeling, into an ineradicable and lifelong passion, but he was thoroughly conscious of a novel and exquisite sensation of supreme contentment, to the charm of which he yielded without reserve, and without troubling himself to inquire its cause. His earnest nature was incapable of half measures, and everything conduced to foster the perilous enchantment of the moment : the sweet thanks of Antonina herself, the boundless gratitude of Demas and Baro, the praise and congratulations of the many who came to chat with the charioteer over the details of the accident and his daughter's escape, and whom

the grateful father took good care to send away
fully impressed with the Thracian's prowess, both
on this and other occasions; the prospect of becoming a soldier, and of some day realizing his
boyish dreams; a confidence in himself that daily
grew stronger, not springing from vanity and
shallowness, but from the intuitive conviction of
noble minds that when the occasion offers they
will not be found wanting. Even the glorious
autumn weather seemed to accommodate itself
graciously to the benign influences which were at
work. In the balmy cool of the evening, when the
air was filled with a soft roseate glow and redolent
with the breath of the reviving flowers, Antonina's
couch would be spread in a sheltered nook of the
garden overlooking the harbour, and never did the
girl show to greater advantage than during these
hours of her convalescence, half sitting, half re-
clining among the shadows of the leaves, her
natural vivacity tempered by a becoming langour,
and her beauty refined by the absence of its super-
abundant roses.

And the Thracian would sit silently by and watch
her, and in his great simple heart thank God with
unselfish fervour that he had been the means of
snatching this fair, delicate creature from the cold
embraces of the Bosphorus. It had not as yet
entered into his head to covet the rescued treasure altogether for himself. The frequent visits

of Paris to inquire after the invalid excited no jealousy or distrust in Belitzar ; he would have been very much pained and disgusted if any one who had known the girl before had not manifested uncommon anxiety and interest about her now.

To suppose that Antonina did not foresee the result of all this would be to deny to her ordinary feminine perspicacity, whereas she possessed that quality in a remarkable degree; but it would have been difficult for her to have altered the position of affairs even had she been disposed to do so. It can hardly be expected of a young woman that she should snub the man who has just saved her life, however much it may be for his good. In plain truth, however, the virgin devotion of the Thracian was a rare offering which no girl of Antonina's character could bring herself to resign. At the same time, although Paris had not yet spoken plainly, there could be little doubt that he would do so before long, and she had made up her mind to marry him. It is, perhaps, best not to be too inquisitive over the wheels within wheels of Antonina's mental mechanism. The undeniable fact remains that she derived intense satisfaction from being watched and tended by the magnificent youth, who, by right of salvage, had acquired a claim to regard her with a tender solicitude that even Paris must have felt himself bound to tolerate, had it been possible for that most unimaginative and self-satis-

fied young aristocrat to conceive the existence of a
rivalry between himself and an obscure Thracian
boatman. But Antonina knew how to manage;
she never pitted these two against each other, feeling quite secure of both. It was only in the absence
of Paris that she would entice the boy to sit beside
her and amuse her with oft-told tales of his forest
home, or feign some excuse for the rearrangement
of her pillows and couch, simply for the pleasure
of marking how deftly his strong brown hands could
adapt themselves to such unwonted functions. Now
and then, when the little serpent felt or pretended
to feel a return of weakness, or a sudden lassitude,
the young giant was fain at her pretty complaint to
lift the slender form in his mighty arms and carry
it reverently and tenderly, not without a strange
fluttering at his heart, back to the house.

"Before you leave us, Prince, we must really
civilize your ancestral name," she said to him,
laughingly, one day. "Belitzar!" with a pouting
emphasis on the jarring consonants—"it is too
harsh and rough for you; you must be called
Belisarius;" and the melodious vowels melted from
her lips in a caressing murmur, like the prelude to
a kiss.

    *   *   *   *   *   *

Before long the day arrived for the wedding of
Hypatius and Maria. We have learnt that, in the
words of Ecebolus, the shame of Theodora was to

be the crowning glory of the occasion. It becomes
necessary to retrace our steps and glance at the
circumstances which led to this miserable result.
Poor Theodora! I confess to a great sympathy
for her, and were I not cheered by the knowledge
that she will at last emerge triumphantly out
of all her troubles and wipe away the degradation
of her early days by her subsequent career, I should
be doleful over the end of this book, which con-
tains the outlines of that degradation.

As Chrysomalla had foreseen, the apprenticeship
of Theodora to the stage was a comparatively easy
affair, and more of a pleasure than a task to both
pupil and mistress. The girl's natural gifts were
so extraordinary, her perception of all that was
graceful and beautiful so keen and true, that her
mere bodily training was soon perfected. Moreover, under judicious treatment her sullenness and
petulance passed off, and she developed a strong
vein of vivacity and humour which charmed her
instructress. Everything, therefore, went smoothly
enough at the girl's first appearances, and, considering her purposely limited opportunities, she
achieved a fair success, principally by her personal
attractions, and a certain playful grace with which
she contrived to invest even the bare buffoonery and
not seldom grossly conceived situations which the
Byzantine taste demanded. But when Chrysomalla
began cautiously to feel her way towards introducing

Theodora to those special phases of the profession to which in her mind she had devoted her, the girl's innate modesty, or pride, or both, took alarm, and up went her back again in resolute defiance of her temptress. In vain did the latter rack her wicked little brains for some device to overcome these scruples. As will be readily understood, there was no lack of bad example among the easygoing sylphs of the theatre, but this, from its professionality and constant repetition, had lost all force. Theodora had by degrees become inured to indelicacy in others, and treated it as a matter of course, though she declined obstinately to descend to their level. Then Chrysomalla tried what ridicule could effect, and set Indara and one or two of her most unscrupulous pets to work to laugh and tease the nonsense out of her, which of course was a failure also. The idea of severity was abandoned altogether; it only soured and hardened the girl, without any profitable result.

"It is incredible," said Chrysomalla, in despair, to her tame Prefect, "how people will stand in their own light. If that girl would only get off her stilts and take a simple step in the right direction, she might be the wonder of the world. And," she added, with venomous experience, "the most cruel part of it is, that in spite of her airs I am convinced she would like it, and has a natural genius for that sort of thing. Don't tell me; I am never mistaken.

Look at her. Do you suppose that face and figure, those eyes and that mouth, were meant to be thrown away upon a prude? No, sir; not one of them all could be so superbly reckless, so audaciously brazen as she could be. Trust those earnest, high-spirited, passionate hussies if they once give way. Ah, if she were but as pliable as that giggling blue-eyed idiot Comito, she might have all Constantinople raving mad about her to-morrow! And to think how the profession loses through her obstinacy! My dear Prefect, we haven't got a girl now who could do Andromeda, say, without looking like an indecent scarecrow or a criminal tied up to be whipped. I could look forward to a serene old age if I could once see Theodora entered for the mythological parts."

Chance and the devil befriended Chrysomalla. One morning, as Theodora was returning from rehearsal, full of indignation at the renewed proposition of the ballet mistress that at the next public performance she should appear in a certain delicately woven and embroidered tunic, which for scantiness and tenuity might have served the purpose of the free-limbed Diana Venatrix, or even the chaste immodesty of a single-garmented Spartan Phænomeris, she found herself in a quiet street following the steps of two females, the one an elderly woman of staid and duenna-like appearance, the other a young girl dressed in a tight

robe of dark grey, with a white veil partially concealing her face. When Theodora was close upon
them the pair turned by a side wicket into the
gardens of a large mansion, and at that moment,
catching a glimpse of the girl's features, she recognized her sister Anastasia. Now, since the reception
of the latter within the pale of Juliana Patricia's
household, the sisters had never met, and therefore
poor Theodora, yearning for a word of sympathy
and affection, after a moment's hesitation plucked
up courage, opened the wicket, and followed them.
But they had already disappeared among the
shrubberies. Theodora hurried on, in her eagerness took a wrong turn, found out her mistake,
hurried back, and got bewildered in the labyrinth
of paths and thickets, from which she emerged
abruptly at a run, to find herself in a trim area
of lawn and flower-bed, where under a tree sat a
very magnificent and very majestic lady, in front
of whom stood Anastasia and her companion, while
a dozen demure-looking handmaidens were seated
round diligently plying their needles, and in the
background a couple of portly statuesque negroes.

"I trust you were attentive to the discourse of
the reverend father," the great lady was saying at
the moment when the hapless Theodora broke into
the decorous circle; and before she could check
herself called out "Anastasia!"

There was a general start.

" Who is this young person ? " inquired the lady, fixing her ox-eyes upon Theodora.

As nobody answered, she had to repeat her question with some asperity.

" It is my sister, madam," faltered Anastasia.

" Your sister! How did she get here ? "

" I saw her turn in out of the street, madam," explained Theodora, very humbly, " and followed, in the hope of speaking to her. We have not seen each other for such a long time. I am very sorry for my intrusion ; I did not think there would be any one here."

" Are you not an actress ? " asked the lady, slowly, and with an indescribable accent on the last word, as though her lips had been forced to mention some unspeakable abomination.

" I am, madam," replied Theodora, rather defiantly, for the tone made her blood stir ; " but I love my sister for all that."

" Shameless girl! " exclaimed the Juno, colouring with wrath, and rising from her seat. " How dare you force your way in here ? "

And to this speech there was a chorus of horrified murmurs from the demure handmaidens, and a prolonged groan from the duenna.

" Remove that consecrated child," continued the lady, addressing the female from whom the doleful sound issued, " from the contamination of her unhappy sister's presence."

And as Anastasia was led away in tears, her mistress beckoned to the negroes.

"See this girl clear of the premises," she said, pointing to Theodora, who stood panting with anger; "and take care that for the future the side gate is locked. Begone, abandoned one! Should you attempt any further communication with your sister, you will repent it. Maidens, attend to your work." And the great dame reseated herself, while Theodora, wringing her small hands and grinding her teeth, was marched off between her sable conductors, and with more than one brutal jest thrust ignominiously into the street.

All that night the poor child lay awake, and the powers of darkness had dominion over her. The morning found her pale, dry-eyed, and full of a terrible resolve.

"Why should I fight against my destiny any longer?" she muttered to herself. "I am shameless, am I, and my presence is contamination? They shall see what I can be."

And when she returned to Chrysomalla she told that wretched schemer, to her intense astonishment, that she was quite willing to wear anything, everything, or nothing, and to do whatever she was bidden, if only the interests of the drama could be thereby advanced; and a few days afterwards drove the rest of the company wild with envy at her gracious reception in the new character. This

UNIVERSITY OF ILLINOIS
LIBRARY

was a fresh source of trouble, and for some little time she was tormented by the savage exultation of her companions over the sudden collapse of Miss Prude. And even Comito, deadly jealous, joined her persecutors. Not being able to deny her success, they did their best to embitter the sweets of it, until Chrysomalla assembled her young ladies and informed them that Theodora was worth the lot of them put together,—that she intended her to have the lead in everything, and that there was a sound whipping in store for any one who by word or deed made herself obnoxious. Then, when she marked the glowing cheeks and sparkling eyes with which after a time her paragon came off the stage, and saw that the poison of public approbation was doing its work, she craftily contrived to feed the girl's newly awakened vanity, treating her with the respect due to an artist, giving her superior advantages in the matter of dressing-rooms and attendants, and in short making her a queen among her comrades.

After this state of things had continued for some time, came the suggestion of the part she was to play in the entertainment furnished to the Factions by Count Hypatius. The details of this had been long arranged, and the piece was in active pre-paration, but Chrysomalla's proposal was deferred until the last possible moment. It was received in a manner which disconcerted even that audacious

little woman. She stepped back in something like
dismay as Theodora threw up her hands and burst
into a fit of laughter—so bitter, fierce, and harsh,
that it hardly seemed to come from the girl herself,
but from some mocking, murderous devil within
her.

"Don't be afraid, my good creature," she said,
jeeringly; "I am not going to strangle you. It will
be enough to put an end to myself one of these days
when I am shamed past endurance. Do you know,
I have been expecting this offer for some time, and
I have watched you not daring to ask me. You are
beginning to be afraid of me, I do believe. For
Count Hypatius's wedding-day? How honoured I
ought to feel! What a climax! How much money
did you say I am to have? Well, it is most liberal;
I shall soon grow rich at that rate. And what is to
be the share of my dear stepmother? And the Green
Faction will be there in force, to see me! Will they
be as generous, think you, to the daughter as they
were to the father? Perhaps you wouldn't mind
letting me see my dress; I know you have had it
ready ever so long, and there can't be much of it.
Why don't you fetch it? Why don't you do something? Why do you stand there staring at me? You
miserable woman! do you think I am going mad?
I have a great mind to—that would baulk you
nicely. Ah, my God! my God! if only I *were*
mad, and all this not reality!" And falling prone

on the couch, she burst into a flood of passionate
tears.

* * * * * *

The wedding took place, and was in every respect
the most perfectly organized thing of the kind that
Constantinople had been blessed with for many a
long day. The fair young bride of Hypatius glided
from the seclusion of her virginal chamber to find
herself the centre of the strange amalgamation of
Christian ceremony and heathen pageantry, which
constituted the nuptials of a fashionable Byzantine
couple. It was little wonder that she shrank
timidly to the side of her soldier husband as the
procession slowly crossed the Agora ; and under the
dancing blaze of the torch-light her pure eyes were
greeted by the extravagantly expressive saltations
of the masquers and mummers who accompanied
the bridal chariot, and her pure ears by their
equally extravagant hymeneal and epithalamic
odes, the prophetic and congratulatory expressions
of which could hardly, by any rendering, however
expurgated, be rendered acceptable to modern
readers.

Besides this, for two whole delightful days there
was unlimited feasting and drinking, and a perfect
glut of entertainment :—satyrs and bacchanals, who
danced upon the tight-rope ; tumblers, male and
female, who turned somersaults over sword-points,
and twisted themselves into a writhing jumble of

heads and limbs; jugglers, wrestlers, fire-eaters, performing animals, sambycistæ, or female harpists, all gauze and spangles; players on the flute, the cymbals, the single pipe, the double pipe, and all kinds of music.

But it was in the theatre that the real cream of the enjoyment was to be found. As the performance lasted half the day we shall transport ourselves thither during only one scene, in company with the male characters of our story, including Ecebolus, Justinian, and Belisarius—for the amendment of Antonina must henceforth be adopted in reference to the Thracian's name.

*　　*　　*　　*　　*　　*

A hush of breathless excitement. Theodora is dancing Hesione. From the lowest tier of the orchestra to the topmost gallery beneath the awning one vast curving bank of eager faces, flushed with the intensity of pleasure. A low symphony, weird, tremulous, and fitful, sobbing and pulsating, swelling and dying, like the far-booming moan of the outer surges, and the pipe of sea-winds vagrant over grassy dunes or through the weed-tresses of caverned headlands.

In the foreground a level platform of rock, and beyond, a spur of cliff descending in ragged ledges to the inky waters of a basin scooped by the churning tide; and further still, above a line of breakers and flat grey shore, a glimpse of towered Ilion and the piny slopes of Ida.

But why do the sea-maidens, uplifting from the wave their white shoulders and dishevelled locks, cling to each other and gaze pitifully upwards, or with mute lamentation pillow their drooped heads upon the rocky margin? They mourn for the new victim to the wrath of their unrelenting lord, Poseidon; for Hesione, the daughter of Trojan Laomedon.

White as the gleaming curl of a moonlit wave, soft as the breast of the sea-bird or the gathered foam, rounded and pliant as the stem of the ocean weed, the exquisite form of the maiden is revealed against the rugged surface of the cliff. Her tender feet tremble on the narrow ledge, her outstretched arms are manacled to the stone, and from her brow, upturned to the pitiless heavens, a veil of chestnut tresses ripples down to mingle with her zone of trailing weed.

A rushing sound as of a mighty billow, or the first blast which heralds the tempest! and the scared Nereids plunge beneath the wave and disappear. The shuddering wail of the music rises to a shriek, and out of the depth of the eddying pool emerge the cruel lidless eyes and horny jaws of the sea-monster.

Slowly he floats towards the doomed princess; slowly, with griding scales, his bulk rears itself against the ledge. In vain the slight wrists struggle against the fetters, vain the lithe terror of that supple form and the agonized shrinkings of the delicate limbs; the horrid jaws gape to seize their prey! Ye gods, have pity!

Hark! the twanging of a bow, the hist of an arrow, and the shaft is seen quivering in the monster's throat. Another, and another! And now, with awful lashings and writhings of his serpent-coils, the Scourge of the Gods drops back into the pool, and Alcides of the lion's hide strides forth upon the scene.

Scoring the rock with his strong talons the baffled monster drags himself forth to meet his foe, but the rooted barbs are spreading the poison of the Lernæan hydra through his blood, and the victory of the hero is half secured.

It is soon complete. Resistless as the bolt of Jove himself, the mighty club descends again and again; the bones crash beneath the swinging brass, and with one last appalling throe the stricken monster rolls plunging off the rock, and settles lifelessly down into the crimsoned waters.

Then in a moment the chorus breaks into a jubilant strain, the air is resonant with the bray of conchs and sea-horns, and headed by the grey-beard Proteus the tritons and nymphs come thronging in.

Tenderly they loose the rescued maiden from her

chains, and bearing her, faint and trembling, to the level rocks, group themselves around her prostrate loveliness.

See! she opens her large eyes, and with a shiver recloses them; again the long lashes steal upwards, and she glances fearfully round. No cavernous maw stifling her with its poisonous breath, no range of glistening fangs; only a circle of kindly, pitying faces between her and the serene blue of heaven, only the pure sea-breeze playing on her cheek.

Returning hope flashes like a sunbeam across her face. Gradually, assisted by the Nereids, she raises herself. Her coral lips part, her snowy bosom heaves in a delicious sigh. It is true; she is saved—saved! And yonder, leaning with knotted arms upon the blood-stained mace, stands her pre-server. With pretty impulsive gratitude she springs erect, and running forward bends to her knee before the smiling Demigod.

Then the music quickens, and with waving arms and filmy draperies floating on the breeze the Nereids begin their dance of joy and triumph. She alone, coyly graceful, innocently nude, stands listening. A thrilling consciousness of deliverance courses through every limb; she feels buoyant as the air or the circumambient waters. Her restless feet beat time to the enticing measure; forgetful of all else, she yields to the delirium of the moment,

and in a chaste ecstasy of subtlest motion proclaims
her sense of rapture and relief.

*   *   *   *   *   *

"Well done, my darling!" cried Chrysomalla,
as with genuine professional enthusiasm she folded
Theodora, flushed and panting, in her arms. "Are
you glad now you took my advice? Here, my
beauty, wrap this round you. Ah, you may well
shout," she continued, apostrophizing the audience,
as the thunder of the repeated plaudits reached
her; "you may well shout. Such a dancer has
not been seen in this city since the day when
Constantine built the theatre."

CHAPTER IX.

LOVE AND PASSION.

THE morning after the great treat in the theatre, Antonina, now restored to perfect health and looking her very best, asked Belisarius a most natural and apparently simple and commonplace question, "How did he like the pantomime?"—in so many words. By which the Thracian was led into expatiating with much animation on the many delights and wonders of the performance, with a special encomium reserved for the concluding scene, the introduction of real water, with real nymphs swimming in it, the gallant behaviour of Hercules, the defeat of the monster, and the generally satisfactory ending.

But this, although it amused her, was not sufficient for Antonina, and she required further particulars, especially about the new dancer. "What did he think of her?" To which again the young man replied by bearing ample testimony to Theodora's grace and activity; her thorough appreciation of the part, as far as he was capable of judging, and her wondrous power of expressing the emotions without the aid of language. All this with the same simplicity and straightforwardness with which he would have given Demas an opinion of one of his thoroughbreds.

Antonina eyed him curiously. "Then you did not fall in love with her?" she said abruptly.

Fall in love with her! Had she said with the monster her question would have been as intelligible to him; so entirely did his rustic naïveness, uncorrupted as yet by his sojourn in the city, disconnect the actress from the sphere of ordinary mortals, and deny to her all association with ordinary flesh and blood. At his age, had the Thracian possessed rather more sentimentalism, he might have idealized Theodora; with less natural refinement he would have animalized her. It was a fair test of the artist's delicacy and purity of conception, that whatever may have been the effect on the feverish artificial appetite of the Byzantines, the clean, healthy palate of the young provincial was not offended by any prurient flavour in the dish set before it. To him the actress was a being born or created out of the exigencies of the stage-world, a piece of perfect mechanism exquisitely adapted to the end in view. Her beauty, symmetry, and skill were so many ingredients in the drama—inherent necessities. The exposure of Hesione, the convul-

sions of the dying monster, the athletic poses of
muscular Hercules, were alike sources of gratification and alike subjects for criticism. It was certainly novel and strange, and to a certain extent
startling at first. But to fall in love with her!
Nay!

Antonina was extremely diverted. The exclamation was to her so comically serious, so full of real
surprise. But she understood him perfectly. A
thrill of delight ran through her as she realized
more completely than ever that with her, and her
alone, rested the power of troubling the tranquil
waters of this young Spartan's soul. How she
admired him!—possibly by virtue of the strong
contrast to herself. She was as near genuine love
at that moment as she ever was in her life.

The temptation to try a little further was irresistible. "Did you not like her?" she asked. "Is
she not lovely?"

"Most lovely," replied the boy, candidly, looking
straight at her.

"And the monster was ugly, I suppose?" said
Antonina, mockingly.

"Hideous!"

The girl burst into a fit of musical laughter. "I
never saw any one at all like you," she protested,
radiant with mirth. "How delightfully matter of
fact you are! Do you think you could really take
a great fancy to any living thing, unless it might

be an old Emperor, or a horse, or a cruel wild
beast?"

This time Belisarius did not answer, but continued looking into her glistening eyes with a
strange yearning expression in his own.

Some voice within warned Antonina to be prudent,
but she was too happy to listen to it.

"Tell me, could you?" she persisted.

He was still gazing earnestly at her. "I think I
could," he replied slowly, in a deep, vibrating tone.

Antonina heard and quivered with the excitement
of imminent victory. "Ah, I cannot believe it,"
she said, shaking her head with sweet pensiveness;
"at all events not to such a poor, frivolous, inferior
thing as a woman." And then she looked up at
him—audacious minx!—and expected the climax.

It came with a vengeance, perhaps rather more
suddenly and decidedly than the temptress anticipated. What was this? What novel sensation was
it, strange and delicious, which set the Thracian's
heart leaping so wildly, and sent the hot blood
surging and singing into his head; while, under
some absorbing spell, the garden, the trees, the
sunshine, sea and sky, everything vanished, leaving
only that fair, rosy face, with its swimming dark
eyes and pouting lips, looking up into his?

Belisarius could never account to himself satis-
factorily for the catastrophe, but all of a sudden he
had caught Antonina in his arms and was covering

her soft face and lips with the first kisses he had ever bestowed on woman, and so committed himself to the one passion of his life.

The girl had triumphed. For a few seconds she lay passive in his embrace, every sense and fibre in her nature yielding to the luscious mesmerism of the boy's ardour, and then her cool intriguing brain came to the rescue.

"No, no!" she panted, struggling to release herself; "let me go. You must; you are mad. I was mad to teaze you so; I did not mean what I said. Let me go, dear, dear boy; let me go, if you care for me one bit," and by this stroke of tenderness she regained her freedom. "Ah, heavens! there is my father!" she exclaimed; and bounding off like a roe, she left the young man standing there pale with emotion, happy to desperation, and ready to confront the whole world on behalf of his new-born love.

But Demas was a wise man, and a kindly one into the bargain. Even if his sharp eyes had not noted the proud, unabashed demeanour of Belisarius as the girl left him, he would have staked his existence on the truth and loyalty of the former; and, while he inwardly resolved that this sort of thing must be nipped in the bud, he acknowledged to himself with rare compassion that he would sooner be beaten on the post in his next race than have to inflict so cruel a stab on a staunch heart

like the young Thracian's, which was admitting a
great deal; and I fear he added a deep curse on
the duplicity and unreliableness of all things
feminine, from mares upwards, and on the folly of
fathers who spoilt and indulged their daughters
until they got out of hand altogether.

But instead of blundering up to Belisarius, who
was about five yards off, and demanding immediate
explanation, he affected to ignore the presence of
any one in a brazen, deliberate fashion that would
have been audacious even in a blind man, and
sauntered whistling in the opposite direction.

Before another hour had gone over her mischievous little head, Antonina was treated to such
a bit of her father's mind as had not fallen to her
lot for many a day; but it was not until the quiet
of the evening, when the Thracian's work was
done, and he was in eager expectation, now that
the ice was fairly broken, of meeting his dear one
again, that the charioteer contrived to get the poor
boy alone, and with reluctant decision annihilated
his ephemeral happiness.

"When a man like myself," said Demas, "whose
eyes are sharp enough to watch a string of gallop-
ing horses and note the length of every stride and
the play of every muscle, catches a young fellow
hugging and kissing his daughter, and walks off
pretending not to see anything, you may be sure
that man has strong reasons for choosing to look

like a fool. And now I'll tell you them. In the first
place, I did it for my own sake; for I'm a little hard
in the mouth when I'm roused, and if I had once
got fairly away, I might have said a great deal that
I should have been sorry for afterwards. Next, for
your own sake, lad. I thought it better to tackle
you when you were cool and quiet, instead of just
after you had been making the running, and were
trembling and panting and all of a lather."

"I am much obliged to you," said Belisarius
gravely, half amused and half perplexed by this
gush of metaphor.

"Don't try and cut in yet, my lad; let me have my
say out. If I am a trifle slow at starting, I shall
come with a rush at the finish. I am going to be
hard upon you, I don't deny it, but if your sort
can't stand a stiffish trial, then breeding and bone
and muscle go for nothing. I shall be hard upon
myself too. Look how much we owe you. But for
you old Baro was a lost man, and that aggravating
hussy would have been lying quiet enough beneath
yonder waves. That's where the gall is. If you
were an outsider like one of those lounging coxcombs, trying to slip their arms round the waist of
every girl who is fool enough to look twice at them,
I should have made short work of it, I promise you.
But you—you—you see —— "

"Whatever you have in your mind to say,"
interrupted the Thracian firmly, "I look to your

saying it without hesitation or reserve, without a thought of any obligation between us. The debt is not all on one side. But for you and yours I should have wandered about a friendless stranger in this great city, and Heaven knows into what trouble and danger."

"Thank you, my lad," said Demas; "you make it a bit easier for me. If, as I was saying, you were like one of those frothy coxcombs, I shouldn't think twice about the matter; but I've watched you. You are honest and staunch; whatever you do, I don't care what it is, you put your heart into it. When you enter for a stake you will run till you drop, and never swerve an inch under punishment. Then, that filly of mine; she has been a wild skittish thing from the time she was foaled; made too much of a pet, you see; has never been properly broken, and seldom felt either curb or whip. She's a sweet thing, though. I can guess pretty well how it has been between you, and I'm sorry for it. If I had not been the biggest ass in creation I should have given you a hint and saved all this. I had it out with that little double-dealing hussy this afternoon, and I shall make her repent it yet."

Belisarius started and turned crimson. "You will not be so cruel or unjust!" he exclaimed. "All blame, if blame there be, rests with me. It was my fault. I never knew how—how much I loved her until that moment, and I lost my head. She must not suffer for my presumption!"

"Gently, gently, my brave lad," said the charioteer, soothing the young giant as he would an excited horse; "wait until you know all. She is my own flesh and blood; I have spoilt her these many years, and I am not likely to be harder upon her now than she deserves. You would not be the man I take you for if you did not try to shield her. Lost your head, did you? It was all your fault, was it? Ah! do you think I don't know them, the little hussies?—with their soft eyes and soft voices and soft ways, making a great strapping fellow feel all of a glow and a tremble, like a racer before the start, and never turning a hair themselves."

"Of that I know nothing," said the Thracian. "I do know that to lose his self-control is a shame to a man, as it is to me. But it is no shame to love as I love Antonina. I have neither position nor fortune, nor any friends but your family; but give me a little hope and a little time, and I think I can do something to merit her love and your esteem. I do not mean to boast, but I have confidence in myself."

Demas looked full into the youth's proud, glowing countenance, and caught his sinewy hand in his own iron clutch. "Summon all your self-control now," he cried; "a curse on the hour when I must ask you to do it! You are a noble fellow, after my own heart. It is better you should learn the worst at once. Within the last week I promised the hand of

Antonina to young Paris, and she has promised
that when he asks her she will marry him. I
expect him here to-morrow."

A deadly, sickening chill struck to the heart of
Belisarius as he heard, and he staggered beneath
the cruel blow. In an instant the whole bitter
truth burst upon him. What a blind fool he had
been! He had judged Antonina's feelings by his
own. Now he came to think of it, was there one
speech, one action of hers, during the whole of their
intimacy, which was incompatible with trusting,
indulgent friendship? Had not he himself gloried
in that friendship, and but for that moment of
inexplicable weakness might have gloried in it still?
Could she help being bright-eyed and soft-voiced,
and so tempting altogether? Was he, after all, no
better than those sensual coxcombs whom Demas
had spoken of? And yet, she had lain quiet in his
arms and let him kiss her. What else could she do,
the fragile, delicate thing? He had hurt her once
before with his rude grasp. And then she called
him dear—that he might let her go; a sweet strat-
agem, that was all; she begged him so hard, and
he would not. Perhaps, like her father, she pitied
him, made excuses for his youth and inexperience,
and was too gentle to be angry. Besides, they were
under obligations to him, and he had been mean
enough to take advantage of that. Not by design,
not in his heart, thank God; but in fact and deed,

and under the influence of that mad, irresistible impulse.

All this flashed across him as he stood grasping the hand of the charioteer in a paroxysm of noble shame and self-reproach, and stifling the extenuating whisper which strove to make itself heard. " She did encourage you, she did lead you on ; remember what even her father said." Never! He would not admit one thought against his love. She could not be so unworthy. It was the suggestion of some base vein within him. There were such in all men.

At last he spoke. His words rather astonished and perplexed the charioteer, who could hardly be expected to follow the workings of the boy's sensitive mind.

"I thank you for your kindness," he said, with dignified humility, " and ask your forgiveness and that of your daughter. You will tell her. I will do so in person when I am able, when I am more master of myself, when I come to say farewell. You can amply discharge any debt there may still be between us by not being harsh with her. I alone am to blame. I swear that I will not be so again. I will respect her as if she were wedded already. I cannot say more now." And he turned away and disappeared in the growing dusk.

Grumbling, swearing, shaking his head, Demas went back to the house. "It beats me," he muttered. "I can see that it cuts the poor lad to the quick, but may I never breast the white cord again if I can make out what he means by taking it like that; seems to think of nothing but my not being hard upon the girl. All his fault indeed! I know better. It is high time Antonina went into double harness, alongside of a steady one like Paris."

This conclusion of the charioteer's was certainly unassailable.

The next day Belisarius kept his word, and went to offer his excuses to Antonina. He did not get far with them. He had scarcely opened his lips before the girl cut him short.

"You shall not ask my forgiveness," she said, impetuously; "it is rather I who must implore yours. You are not able to understand how badly I have behaved."

The young man smiled sadly. "It is your kindness and forbearance which makes you accuse yourself," he said. "There is no real reason for it."

"There is, there is!" reiterated the girl, with passionate emphasis. "If you knew more about us—about girls, I mean—you would see that. As it is, you must feel that I did all I could to tempt you and make you care for me. You made me happier than I have ever been in my life in—in—some ways; but I had no right to tempt you—not you; you are so unlike other people, so pure and earnest and truthful. I have always meant to marry Paris; I knew he wanted me to, long, long before he spoke to father, and I ought to have told you. You used to tell me everything; but then I saw how much you liked me, and I felt I could make you very fond of me, if I chose. I could not resist trying, it was so pleasant. But after a while I determined to be open with you. I did indeed, do believe me."

The Thracian bowed his head. He could not trust himself to speak.

"Then came that accident with the boat, and you saved my life. That spoilt everything. All my good resolutions came to nothing. I am afraid they generally do. All I can say to you now is, do not think of me any more. I am not worth it. I am vain, heartless, ambitious. I want to be a lady, to belong to the grand world, and go to court. I dream of that more than of anything else. It is not entirely my fault; I have always been encouraged in the idea of being able to buy a proper husband. Ah! no wonder you are horrified. I can hardly bear to see you look like that, after— after—everything; you would pity me if you knew how much it costs me to tell the truth to you. But it must be done. The more you dislike me now the better. I shall marry Paris, and there will be an end of it."

"But surely you care for him?" asked the boy,

hoarsely. For the life of him he could not repress the question.

Antonina gulped down a sob. "Will you never understand? Yes, yes; I like him very much. In some ways he resembles you. He, too, is brave and honourable, and—and—he thinks me quite perfect. I am not sure that I can really love; I think I only admire. It is so difficult to explain. You must not ask me any more. You are going to leave us and become a soldier. You will rise to rank and wealth one of these days—I am certain of it—and will forget me altogether. If ever we meet again you will laugh at yourself for having been so stupid as to care about me. Perhaps, when you learn all, and have more experience of women, you may hate and despise me."

Antonina was doing her very best to be sincere, but sincerity was foreign to her nature. She could not help being affected by her own pretty pleading against herself, and felt all the while that it was very becoming.

"You know that to be utterly impossible," interrupted Belisarius, with indignation; "or that I can ever forget you. You are far more likely to forget that there is such a person as myself in existence."

"When you saved my life!" exclaimed Antonina, reproachfully. "I have made you a poor return, but I am not quite so bad as that. I wish you to forget

me or to hate me, because in the end it will be the
better for you. You will find some one to make
you a thousand times happier than I should. But
I shall always think of you as a dear friend, and
love to recollect that I have known any one so good
and brave and true-hearted."

She was sobbing openly now, and the large tears
were running down her cheeks. The boy's heart
yearned towards her, but he mastered himself and
went on calmly—

"Your new life will allow little room for such
recollections. It is not fair to expect it. But I
will school myself into thinking of you as—as I did
before yesterday ; into picturing you just as you
used to be, when you seemed to feel an interest in
all I had ever done, and in all I hoped to do for the
future. I had not found out how dear you were to
me ; but I had a fancy, a dream, that if ever I succeeded in making my name heard for good, you
would be pleased, and that your pleasure and
your approbation would be worth the praise of the
whole world. I shall still cling to that dream, vain
as it may be. It is not a great deal, after the
hopes I have dared to indulge within the last few
hours, and have now to relinquish ; but, true or
false, it will comfort me, and I wrong no one by it."

Then in her turn she lost her head, and springing
at him tried to throw her arms round his neck ; but
he caught the slender wrists and held them fast, as

much a hero in resisting that frail girl as when in later years he confronted the spears of the Immortals and the Gothic broadswords.

"Yes," she cried, "you wrong yourself! You shall not relinquish everything for a mere shadow! If you care so much for me, take me! They shall let me marry you and make you rich. Ah, that is no temptation for you. But I am; take me! Whatever happens, I will submit to it for your sake. I can be brave too. Rich or poor, I will follow you; and by your side I will shrink from nothing. Take me! You saved me. I belong to you. I am your property. Take me; and do what you like with me! Kiss me, darling! kiss me again, as you did before!"

But he stood firm, and held her away from him. There was real danger, and his growing manhood, his rare nerve and resolution, rose up against the temptation as against a material enemy.

"As God is above us," he said solemnly, "I hold you as much the property of another as if the Church had joined you. You have given your promise; your father has given his, and will never go back from his word. I have sworn to him to respect you as if you were a wife, and I cannot be false to my oath. My honour and your happiness are at stake. I would lay down my life at your feet; I will consecrate it to your memory, but I will not accept the sacrifice of yours. You have told me too much. I will not bring you to curse the hour when you linked yourself to the fortunes of a selfish adventurer."

She was quiet now, listening with wonder to his steadfast accents. He had expanded from an ardent, love-stricken boy into a thoughtful, chivalrous man.

"Say good-bye, then," she whispered; and he freed her wrists, sighing to himself as he noted the red circles left upon that tender skin by his restraining hold. Then he held out his hand. She caught it, bent over it, and pressed it to her bosom until he could feel the throbbing of her heart, cast one glance up at his yearning, resolute face, and then, with a sudden gesture, almost threw his hand from her, and walked silently away.

CHAPTER X.

BIRDS OF A FEATHER.

John of Cappadocia had returned, as it is said men always do, to his first love, the once cherished idea that a grand destiny awaited the family of Acacius, or, at least, some member of it. This fancy had engaged the earliest affections of his scheming brain, and was now the object of its maturer passion for intrigue. Not that he meditated rebuilding any serious hopes on so precarious a foundation, but having for the time being no more important matter to occupy his hours of leisure, he determined to devote them to following up the clue which at length seemed to have revealed itself. This he set himself to do more as a pastime than a task. Whether he succeeded or failed in obtaining any sterling result was a matter of comparative indifference to him, now that his position in the world was established on the solid basis of a government appointment and a large salary. For

since the escape of the Emperor Anastasius during
the sedition, John's merits had received further
recognition from the authorities, and he was pro-
moted to be head of a department under the
Prætorian Prefect, an important and highly paid
post, the emoluments of which, in the way of fees,
perquisites, and donatives, might be indefinitely
increased, according to the ingenuity and industry
of the holder. He could afford to indulge in the
luxury of an exciting, although it might be a barren,
quest. There was just sufficient chance of profit
to stimulate him into exertion, and there was a
minimum of risk. Ah! the relief of playing spy
and meddling in the concerns of other people,
purely on his own account; of being freed from
the constant dread of detection and exposure!
The more he thought of it the more he revelled
in the idea; he had discovered a new pleasure.

It must be confessed that it required a very
sanguine disposition and a very acute discernment,
with a rare confidence in the omnipotence of
destiny, to detect even the faint vestige of a track
across the wilderness of improbability, which inter-
vened between the present position of Theodora and
anything like an honourable, much less a glorious,
future. The higher she rose in her present calling
the lower she was likely to sink in the estimation
of all decent society; and the Cappadocian could
not conceal from himself that to achieve the ignoble

triumph of being a queen among pantomimists and courtesans, or even to culminate as the honoured Hetæra of a great man—even as Aspasia of old—could hardly be accepted as a fulfilment of the starry prognostications.

The very starting-point of John's calculations was a notion to all appearances supremely absurd and anomalous. And yet it was this very absurdity and anomaly which caught the Cappadocian's fancy, coinciding as it did with his belief in a mysterious and supernatural influence.

Nothing could be more wildly improbable, more opposed to all reason and common sense, than the supposition that Justinian, the immaculate, the ascetic, the student, the faster, the pattern of all that was virtuous and orthodox, the hope and desire of the Blue Faction, could entertain any species of admiration, much less affection, for the dancer with whose scandalous success all Constantinople was ringing, whose degrading pre-eminence was the glory of the Green Theatre, whose name was a toast for every group of carousing ruffians and a theme for every ribald ballad, and whose undraped perfection was now as familiar to half the population as the brazen horses above the Baths of Zeuxippus. The thing was all but inconceivable ; and yet of the truth of this monstrous improbability, John, by patient observation and diligent repetition of the synthetical process, known as " putting this and that together," at which no one was a greater adept, had managed to convince himself.

It would be wearisome to attempt to analyze the numerous points of evidence by which the Cappadocian had arrived at this conclusion; points individually trifling and insignificant, but collectively of irresistible weight.

Ever since the moment when, during the conversation at the Villa Ecebolus, the germ of the idea had budded in his mind, he had been more or less occupied in its development. He could not shake off the fancy, and, after some futile efforts to ridicule himself out of it, settled steadily down to its investigation. The process was tedious and the progress slow, but the daring and rapidity which frequently characterized the conception of the Cappadocian's schemes was not more striking than the infinity of perseverance bestowed upon their elaboration. No man ever illustrated better the truth of the saying that genius is patience—the capacity for taking infinite pains.

John had contrived with marvellous tact to ingratiate himself with Justinian, in spite of the latter's half hostile reserve; had studied profoundly every change of expression on his countenance when at the theatre; had noted and weighed every word which escaped his lips upon the one subject. Like a skilful analyst who suspects the presence of some subtle and hitherto undetected element, he set himself to prepare a series of delicate tests to penetrate the secret of Justinian's inmost soul, and in each experiment had found the result to corroborate, however slightly, his suspicions. Lastly, as his official duties occupied the best part of his time, he felt the necessity for providing himself with an agent who might in some measure supply the place, and discharge the functions of the deceased Acacius. Here fortune befriended him by throwing in his way the ex-chorister Isidore, who, his voice having at length failed him, found to his disgust that his eminent services on behalf of the Imperial heresy were entirely overlooked, and that he was generally regarded as a rowdy hireling, a promoter of discord, and an objectionable kind of person altogether. To this man, whose coolness and audacity were valuable qualities in a spy, John determined to entrust the task of watching the movements of Justinian; intimating to him that such employment was not unconnected with political intrigue, and that any indiscretion on the part of Isidore might result in his abrupt disappearance from society, while secrecy and zeal would be regularly and liberally rewarded. Much impressed with the importance of his mission, Isidore set to work with a will, and from the mass of trivial and worthless rubbish which composed his daily report John was able to extract two pieces of intelligence, which fully repaid him for his outlay. The first

was this: Justinian, who for some time past had
never been seen in the theatre, had nevertheless
been detected on two occasions watching, alone and
cloaked from head to foot, Theodora's exit from her
own apartments on her way to some supper-party
given by one or other of her aristocratic patrons.
On these occasions the actress seemed to take a
special delight in scandalizing the respectable
portion of Byzantine society by the ostentation
of her progress, and in taxing to the utmost the
forbearance of the sumptuary laws affecting women
in her condition. As she passed through the
streets, the torches of her attendants flashed upon
the splendid appointments of her litter, and the
lustrous silks and gems which lavishly decorated
the person of its fair occupant.

There, then, at last was the decisive proof which
the Cappadocian had so long been seeking, and he
was able to congratulate himself on his unerring
perspicacity. There was clearly a struggle going on
between Justinian's principles and impulses. He
studiously avoided the sight of Theodora in public,
but he could not resist the temptation of catching
a glimpse of her on the sly. Where another would
have gone boldly to work and make her acquaintance, the student and ascetic hung back, ashamed
and terrified at his own weakness—to which he
nevertheless yielded. The immaculate one was
after all not without spot, the pattern of abstemi-

ousness possessed commonplace human appetites. Truly a pitiable discovery!

But the second point was almost as curious and more puzzling. The movements of Justinian were evidently being watched by some one else besides Isidore. In whose interest and for what purpose, was the question. From the ex-chorister's account there could be no doubt of the fact. More than once his ingenuity had been sorely tried to avoid a collision with the rival supervisor.

The next consideration was, what was to be the issue of all this? To what profitable end could the information be turned? Would it be feasible to establish any hold upon Justinian — to curry favour with any one else? Or were events actually tending to consummate the destiny of the Cyprian's family? If this madness—for it was nothing less—could seize upon a man like Justinian, how far would it carry him? In most men such a fancy would be a thing of comparatively little importance, a mere by-play; but in him it was a reversal of every principle, a stultification of the whole tenor of a lifetime. In what light would he be likely to regard one who had penetrated his weakness, and came to his assistance either to foster it or to save him from it? As one to be trusted or repulsed—as friend or enemy? There were so many views to take of the matter, and none too extensive or too narrow, too daring or too contemptible, for the Cappadocian to entertain.

Then as to Theodora. She was another enigma.
All Constantinople was in a ferment over her. Not
a day passed but some new anecdote of her regaled
the scandal-mongers and tattlers of the city.
More than half of these were probably inventions,
but the authenticated residue made a marvellous
collection. It was strange that when people came
to compare notes no two could agree about her,
except that she was perfectly beautiful and graceful,
and an incomparable dancer. On these points all
were as yet unanimous. But as to her private
character and qualities they were all at sixes and
sevens. According to one account she was a fallen
angel, retaining much of celestial excellence in her
fall; according to another she was an incarnate
demon, equally retentive in another fashion. She
was high-spirited, warm-hearted, generous; simple
in her personal habits, and devoted to her profession. No; she was heartless, vindictive, luxurious, and of sharklike rapacity. She was sullen,
ill-tempered, and insolent, and vivacious only on
the stage; on the contrary, she was sprightly,
affable, and courteous to all, even the meanest.
She was cold-blooded, ambitious, cruel, and deliberately licentious. By no means; she was a
creature of impulse, and the victim of circumstances, ardent and melting as the Cyprian goddess
herself.

It was stated on the best authority that Ecebolus

the Tyrian had offered her the title-deeds of one of
the most charming houses in Constantinople, which
he had purchased and furnished in the costliest
manner from basement to garret, and that she had
scornfully rejected the gift and tossed the title-deeds
in his face. On the other hand it was affirmed,
with equal positiveness, that some one of the many
aspirants to her favour had bought for her, at her
express desire, the dingy, miserable tenement in
which her father, Acacius, had died; though what
she intended to do with such a loathly den no one
could possibly imagine.

John of Cappadocia might be termed a credulous
man on some points, but on the whole he was wont
to observe the excellent rule of believing nothing
that he heard and only half of what he saw. He
knew that for the present Theodora occupied a
suite of apartments in Chrysomalla's house, and it
was obvious that the shortest method of obtaining
information about the actress was to pay a visit to
the little ballet-mistress, with whom he had scraped
an acquaintance, as with most people, and to match
his wits against hers. Not that Chrysomalla was
in the least more likely to speak the truth than any
one else, but John had a profound belief in his own
sagacity and experience, in his power of sifting the
few grains of wheat out of any given quantity of
chaff.

And accordingly one morning we find him closeted

with the little pink and white woman, sustaining
with exemplary energy a brisk commonplace conversation, and feeling his way cautiously to the
introduction of more interesting topics.

"I would give something to know the real object
of your coming to see me," said Chrysomalla all
of a sudden, putting her head on one side with her
most robin-like expression.

"My dear madam, is it necessary to imagine
any other object than the pleasure of enjoying your
society?" replied the Cappadocian, gallantly.

"Of course it is. Do you take me for a simpleton,
sir? You are an extremely pleasant man to chatter
with for half an hour; I don't mind telling you that.
I often say to the Prefect when he makes himself
unusually agreeable, 'Come, what is it? Life is
short and I am in a good humour; you had better
get it off your mind and have done with it.'"

"Fortunate Prefect!" exclaimed John, smiling,
although he was a little nonplussed at this playful
abruptness. "Happy man! to be able to inspire
such interest and to receive such encouragement."

"Interest—hem! Curiosity is nearer the mark.
I am candid, you see. You are welcome to the encouragement, if it does you any good. So again I
ask, what do you want of me? Something, I'll
be bound. Don't be ashamed of it; you cannot
tell how many people in this city want something
of Chrysomalla."

"Dear lady," said John, entering into the little woman's humour, "I will be as open with you as you are with me. Your penetration is not deceived. I have a favour to ask; that you will answer a few questions respecting Theodora."

"Theodora! Theodora?" reiterated Chrysomalla, looking at him sharply. "You don't mean to tell me that?—"No," she added, correcting herself after a moment's thought; "I remember now what Lysias said. You have had something to do with her and her sisters before now."

"Exactly."

"Let me see; how much do I know?" said Chrysomalla, beginning to count upon her fingers. "There was somehow an understanding between you and their father, Acacius. You chose to predict—God knows why—a splendid fortune for him and his family; you promised him on his deathbed that the girls should appear as suppliants; you were kind to them in their trouble;" and here Chrysomalla, having arrived at the little finger, paused. "That is all I actually know, but I could guess a good deal if it wasn't rude," she added slyly.

"Pray do not be deterred by any such consideration; you will embolden me. I shall retaliate by asking all kinds of questions."

"Mind, I make no promise as to answering them. However, I feel good-natured, and we shall see.

The fact is, my dear sir, I have a sort of sympathy with you; I admire you. You are like me in some ways. Whatever you do you have an eye to business. What an impudent woman I am, talking to a Prætorian secretary in this fashion! But don't be offended; it is only my way; nobody minds me. I won't guess. I will begin by asking a question myself. May I?"

"By all means," acquiesced John, blandly.

"Then tell me, did you really believe in your own prophecies about Acacius and his family?"

"Hem! Tell me first how you came to know anything about it."

"Lysias heard it in some way through Hermia."

"Lysias? That is the fellow who has married that fearful woman, Acacius' widow?"

"The same. Have you ever met her?"

"I had that misfortune once, and then she had as narrow an escape from sudden death as may well be."

"Ah! I know when you mean; the night Acacius died. I have heard all about it. So you were present then? Yes, she had a sharp lesson, but I am afraid she has quite forgotten it by this time."

"How is she going on?"

"Worse and worse; to the bad altogether. And Lysias too. Her violence and viciousness drives him wild, and he has taken to drinking. Some-

thing terrible must happen one of these days. I
never dare to let either of them in."

"Beasts and idiots!" exclaimed John with
savage scorn; "the sooner the world is rid of them
both the better!" At this period the Cappadocian
was thoroughly in earnest in his hatred and
contempt of people who allowed their weaknesses
to ruin them.

Chrysomalla took no notice of this little outbreak.
"It must have been convenient," she said dryly,
"when your grand schemes came to nothing, to
carry out poor Acacius' dying wish."

"I was under a solemn oath to do so," replied
John, sonorously.

"I know that; but still I say it must have been
convenient. Now, I own I am burning with curiosity. Have you any hopes left, or is your faith
quite dead?"

"I might ask a long price for relieving you from
torture," said John, smiling, "but I only require
inviolable secrecy."

"The very hardest terms you could propose to
most women; but practice has made discretion
easy to me."

"Know, then," said John, with intense gravity,
"that my faith still breathes."

"Is that all?" said Chrysomalla, discontentedly.

"If you reflect, dear lady," said John, "you will
see that under the circumstances it is a great deal."

"Well, perhaps you are right. What can you be expecting? I suppose, now, you would hardly reckon Theodora's rising to be the head of her profession and making plenty of money of much account. You prophets always fly so high."

"The involutions of incident are too intricate to be followed by human intelligence. We can only argue from broad principles. Hence that which appears to us an insurmountable obstacle may be in truth a stepping-stone to a grand fortune."

"Ah, just so," assented Chrysomalla, rather dubiously. "There is a great deal of truth in that fortune-telling sometimes. I have heard the Prefect say that when Zeno the Isaurian was only a peasant boy, some astrologer predicted that he would be Emperor, and it came true, you know."

"The stars cannot lie," replied the Cappadocian, using one of his pet formulas; "their language only requires proper interpretation. But now it is my turn. I want to learn something about Theodora. There are so many stories abroad. What is she really like?"

"In what way?"

"In every way, or any way. Enumerate her chief characteristics."

"My good sir," said Chrysomalla, opening her round blue eyes, "have you by any chance a week's holiday, and do you mean spending it here? You might as well ask me to enumerate the chief

characteristics of all the statues between this and
the Golden Gate, or of the Agora on a gala day.
You must really narrow your question."

"Is she so versatile ? Well, has she any ambition beyond the theatre ? Does she really care for
aught besides gold, jewels, fine clothes, and unlimited admiration ? besides luxury and sensuality ?
Now, I mean. I know what she was, I can imagine
what she might have been; I wish to find out
what she has become or is becoming."

"If you want to know so much," said Chrysomalla, quickly, "you had better renew your
acquaintance with her, or ask the stars. I am no
prophet. I consider myself a tolerably shrewd
woman, but she utterly bewilders me. You cannot
count on her being the same for two days together.
Sometimes I think that I have made a dancer out
of a saint, sometimes out of a devil."

"Pray don't stop," said John; "your description
is most graphic. Illustrate her saintly tendencies."

"She is as charitable as Juliana Patricia herself,
and makes no fuss over it. Every beggar in the
city knows her and blesses her. She never forgets
a kindness. If you only knew the hundred plans
that girl has devised for helping Hermia ! She
sent her presents openly at first, but the old fool
refused them with floods of tears ; she called them
the wages of sin. Bah ! All our supers adore her :
painters, carpenters, scene-shifters, call-boys, every

one of them. She wheedles all their domestic
secrets out of them, about their sick children, and
wives in the straw, and lame brothers, and delicate
sisters, and helps them all. When Rosamund was
taken ill she nursed the poor child herself, and
sent her at her own expense to Sigæum for change
of air."

"She must be rich," said John.

"You would say so, indeed, if you saw the
presents that come pouring in day after day:
money, plate, jewels, silks, china, mules—— "

"What can she do with them all? Mules, for
instance, are rather bulky tokens of affection."

"Ah! but they fetch a long price—the good ones.
A pair of cream-coloured Caucasians, such as were
given to her the other day, are worth five hundred
gold pieces. She keeps the money and whatever
she has a fancy for, and sells the rest. She never
pretends to sentiment, and takes good care to let
every one know it; but, bless you, it makes no
difference; they are all raving mad about her."

"And who is her agent in these delicate little
transactions?"

"Alexander, the Greek merchant in the Agora.
You know him, of course. Now, there is another
curious thing; he did her some service once; what
it was I don't know."

"Lent her money, probably; far-seeing old
rascal."

" I don't believe that was it; but it doesn't matter.
He seldom comes here without bringing some
ornament or other for approbation, and she always
buys it. The other day he brought a bracelet—a
gold monster with an emerald in its head—a model
of the sea-beast in the pantomime. She buys it, of
course. A week after, when she was dancing, the
emerald drops out and is lost. 'Do you care about
having this, Chrysomalla?' says my lady, with her
grand air. 'It is of no use to me now; you had
better keep it.'—Stay, I will show it to you; it is
worth fifty gold pieces as it is, without the stone."

And out of a small casket on the table beside
her Chrysomalla produced the bracelet in question.
She opened and reclosed the lid with a caution
which seemed to the Cappadocian both awkward
and unnecessary. " There is something in there
that she is afraid of my seeing," he said to himself.

" It is beautifully chased, is it not?" inquired
Chrysomalla; " every scale perfect," as John twisted
the flexible body of the monster round his large
fingers.

" Exquisitely. And the emerald, you say, was
lost?"

" Somebody picked it up, of course. I searched
the whole place myself."

" A thousand pities! And out of all these
stricken idiots you speak of, is there any one she
prefers to the rest?"

"There is one man she cares for; and that one, I firmly believe, she would banish from her sight if she were able."

"He naturally refuses to be banished?"

"Ay; and more than that, she cannot bring herself to be repellant enough. I doubt if any woman could with him."

"Ecebolus the Tyrian, of course. Is it true he has bought that house for her and that she refused it?"

"Quite true. And mark my words, she will accept it before long. I shall be sorry enough to lose her, for, as you may imagine, she is a lodger worth having."

"And the other miserable place where her father died?"

"She bought that herself. For what purpose I can't say. I believe that she goes there occasionally quite alone; but though I am no coward I dare not speak to her on the subject, and that's the truth. I did once, and—and——"

"She gave you a specimen of the Satanic phase of her character?" said John, as Chrysomalla checked herself.

"Well, she was angry. But that is not what I meant by her being a devil sometimes."

"What, then?"

"I shall tell you no more. I don't see how I can. You must know plenty of scandal about her."

" But it may not be true."

" Some of it is sure to be. Anyhow, sir, you must be content with it."

John sat still playing with the bracelet. "You would not lend me this toy, I suppose?" he asked.

" Well, that is rather a cool request. Do you want to borrow fifty gold pieces?"

" Not in the least. I want this monster with a hole in his head."

" What on earth for?"

" To bait a trap with. Does that excite your curiosity? You shall not lose in the end, I promise you. And in the mean time, if you were to search again carefully, you might find the emerald." And John glanced meaningly at the casket.

" You think so, do you?" said Chrysomalla, impudently. " Now, supposing that I agree, and you catch anything in your trap, you will not forget me? Men are so faithless."

" I swear to you that I will not. Shall we go a step further and conclude an alliance on the spot? We understand and might be of infinite use to each other."

Chrysomalla peered at him. " I wonder if you are to be trusted? You are so very deep. I don't relish the idea of being squeezed and sucked like an orange, and then tossed away."

John smiled as his keen eyes ran over the little woman's smooth, doll-like face and comfortable exterior. "Your appearance and surroundings, dear lady, do not suggest your having ever experienced such treatment; why anticipate it now?"

"It is true," replied Chrysomalla, with placid satisfaction, "that I am generally able to take care of myself." And she glanced coquettishly at a neighbouring mirror.

John stretched out his hand, caught up the casket, and deliberately opened it. "This is really a fine stone—a genuine Scythian, I'll be bound," he said, producing from the box the lost emerald, and coolly refitting it to the cavity in the monster's head.

Chrysomalla actually blushed crimson; but her momentary shame and anger evaporated in a laugh. "Your assurance is delicious," she said. "I excuse you this time for your cleverness, but I warn you I shall not tolerate such inquisitive rudeness for the future. Who can tell where you might stop? However, I consent; let us be friends and allies;" and she held out her hand.

John received it into his own massive palm, and applied his lips audibly to the plump bejewelled fingers.

"Hark!" said Chryosmalla, starting up and running to the window; "I hear wheels. Here comes the handsomest man in the world, I'll be bound. Yes, look! What lovely horses! Ah!" she sighed, as Ecebolus disappeared through the

doorway leading to Theodora's apartments, " I
fear I am about to lose my lodger. I have a pre-
sentiment that to-day will settle the matter."

" Under the circumstances," said John, re-seat-
ing himself, " it would be instructive, as well as
advantageous, to know what those young people
have got to say to each other."

" For shame ! " exclaimed Chrysomalla, coquettishly. " Talk about female curiosity ; men are
twice as bad."

" Dear lady, I never indulge in mere curiosity,"
said John ; " it is a petty, dangerous vice. But, as
you accurately observed, I always have an eye to
business. In that light, one cannot know too much
of one's neighbour's affairs. I confess to longing
on this occasion for the facilities of Dionysius."

" And who may he be ? "

" He was an old Greek, who was endowed by art
with an extraordinary gift of hearing. He was
enabled to listen to a conversation carried on
between four solid walls."

" I remember the story now."

" The utility of such a gift is obvious ; so obvious
that I should not be surprised if others, who have
the opportunity, endeavour to rival the ingenious
faculty of the Syracusan."

As he said this, the Cappadocian fixed his eyes
with brazen interrogation on the actress.

" What a man you are ! " said Chrysomalla,

after sustaining the look for some seconds. " I really believe that you are a magician, as people declare, and have dealings with the devil. It cannot be all guesswork. And your shamelessness exceeds mine. Well, we are friends and allies now. I suppose I must humour you. Come with me."

Passing through several rooms, Chrysomalla led the way to one which was decorated with panels. Part of the woodwork yielded to her push, and slid noiselessly back, disclosing a closet hollowed out of the thickness of the wall and softly carpeted. With her finger on her lips Chrysomalla entered, beckoning to John to take his place beside her. In a second voices became clearly audible in the next apartment.

CHAPTER XI.

DÆMONODORA.

"It is certainly incredible that you should be the same Theodora whom I remember as a poor little suppliant at the Cynegium."

"Nor am I; I am quite another person. How dare you remind me again of those days?"

"Did you not tell me you wished never to forget them?"

"There are some things one may have reasons for never forgetting, and yet not choose to be reminded of. Have I not thanked you sufficiently? Do you expect me to make more pretty speeches about your conduct on that occasion?"

"I might be pardoned if I did; they come so sweetly from your lips. But, on the whole, I do not think much of my conduct. Had I but taken a little more than ordinary pains to find out the truth about you——"

"You would have done no good. I was doomed.

I think it a good deal to your credit to have forgotten all about me. You did; don't deny it. Granted that I was only a poor little suppliant; I was very pretty and very friendless, and you had a claim on my gratitude. But everything you did for me then you did purely and disinterestedly— even to the kiss you gave me. You are the only man I ever met whose generosity and tenderness were spontaneous and without some base motive. I suppose I have been thrown amongst very bad people; but so it is. And you risked your life for me. If I can, I want to repay you now."

"Nothing is easier. The accumulation of interest on that kiss alone must be enormous. I am a usurer. Pay me."

"A million of mine now would not repay that one of yours. No amount of stage tinsel is worth a single gem."

"I object to the simile; but, for the sake of argument, I admit it. It is simply a question of one's fancy and demand for tinsel. Mine is unlimited. What have you got there?"

"Do you remember giving me this chain?"

"Of course I do. And you have it still! By what miracle did it escape its natural fate?"

"Being sold, you mean? It was sold, in spite of my grief and anger, my tears and entreaties."

"Poor child! Then you were vexed at having to part with it?"

"Vexed is not the word. I was furious."

"And yet you must have foreseen the calamity. I did."

"So did I. But when it came to the point I rebelled. It maddened me to see my stepmother pouncing with savage greediness, like a vulture, on that which had been given me with such pleasant words and looks. Besides, it was my first present, and after all I was only a foolish, wilful child. I know better now."

"Indeed. And yet you took the trouble of recovering it?"

"To keep faith with myself and the jeweller who bought it. I watched, and found him out, and made him promise never to part with it. I swore to him that I would redeem it some day."

"And you managed to persuade him!"

"Yes. He was naturally a good deal surprised, and very incredulous; but at last he did promise. And he has had no reason to repent of having kept his word."

"That I can believe. What is his name? He deserves patronage."

"He has yours already, I fancy; Alexander, in the Agora."

"I should think he had, indeed. I know him a trifle too well, perhaps. Did he drive a hard bargain with you?"

"He drove none; and when I redeemed the

chain, instead of demanding interest, threw in a great many charming speeches."

"The old fox! He is a genius, though, in his line. And is it possible that some recollection of the donor mingled with your regret at losing the bauble?"

"It seems to me that I have confessed as much. .But don't look too pleased. I have more to tell you. I keep this chain now to mark a crisis in my life. I can show you several things which serve the same purpose—that old sword, for instance, which hangs against the wall. I look at them every day. You would hardly suspect me of being methodical; but I am, terribly so—terribly, in more senses than one. With this chain is associated the remembrance of much that is bitter and something that is sweet. It reminds me of a double debt—of hate and gratitude. It reminds me that for ten minutes of my life a man freely devoted to me his strength, courage, beauty, generosity—all that was noblest in him—and that I can best repay him now by bidding him find something better to do with his manhood than waste it on me."

"Waste it on you! Now it is you who are fishing for compliments. To what better end can it be devoted than in giving you—may I say it without vanity?—a moment's gratification?"

"I can excuse the vanity; but you cannot say it without consummate folly. How?—a thousand

ways. Your beauty was better employed when it
comforted poor little Anastasia in the midst of her
troubles, and gave her something to prattle about
for days after. It is better employed each time
that it causes in any living creature a thrill of
innocent pleasure—even when the very beggars
forget to whine for alms, that they may bless God
for having made anything in human shape so
fair ! ''

" Am I to feel flattered or affronted by all this ?
You certainly are mingling the bitter with the sweet
this morning."

"I have been thinking a great deal last night.
I will tell you more still. Your courage was a
thousand times better employed when you dragged
that loathsome cripple from underneath the horses'
feet than when you defended me at the Cynegium.
I tell you that you had better, for your own sake and
mine—but above all for your own—have caught at
the nearest dagger and stabbed me ; or have left
those villains to insult and outrage me until I
killed myself before them."

" And deprived Constantinople of its greatest
treasure ! "

" God's mercy ! I want you to be serious, and
you pay me empty, vapid compliments. You might
leave others to do that. And yet, if you never
went beyond them, I should be well pleased. I
know why you speak thus. You are too fond of

me ; my present mood troubles you, and you scarcely
know what to say. You will go back to the old
strain before long. Be wise, Ecebolus ; never go
back to it. See me as I am, as all the world sees
me—as the cleverest actress, the most perfect
dancer, the most beautiful animal that has ever
delighted Byzantine eyes—and be content. Admire
me, be amused by me, and go your way."

"I cannot. The actress and the dancer I dis-
regard altogether; I care only for the woman."

"I am no longer woman, I am only female. I
cannot belong to one, for I am in bond to a multitude. There is a compact between me and the
public. All my gifts of body and mind are pledged
to it. It yields me applause, wealth, luxury, makes
an idol of me—a shameful, shameless one, but
still an idol—and in return I give myself."

" No, never ; not your whole self ! not your heart,
your love ! Ah, dearest ! only yield those to me,
and I will make you confess that you have never
been idolized before."

" My heart !—my love ! As if I had any to give
now ! It is too late to talk to me of such things.
I could no more love now than I could cry. I shed
my last tears the night I knew I was to dance
Hesione for Count Hypatius, and then the fountain
dried up. My nature is changed. I was born to
be an angel, I am becoming a fiend ; I was born to
be a blessing, I am becoming a curse ! "

"Hush, hush! for God's sake, Theodora! It is terrible to hear you speak thus."

"It is terrible because it is true. I will speak. I will try to save you from yourself and me. See now what I was, what I am, what I shall be. I *was* Theodora, the daughter of Acacius the Cyprian— the man who devoted his life to the Green Faction; whom it wronged, crushed, and deserted; whom I saw die, through their treatment, broken-hearted and a beggar. I *was* Theodora, who beside my father's death-bed was driven to protect myself with his sword against my stepmother; who, after my supplication for pity had been rejected with insult and scorn, was given back to that brutal woman to be forced on to the stage—a victim to her cruelty and avarice; who, clutching in despair at the last tie which connected me with anything innocent, found my very presence an abomination to the most pious lady in this city, and was turned like a dog into the street. I *am* Theodora, the actress! who, to grace the wedding of the man who had insulted her, to gratify the Faction which rejected her, to bring gain to the woman who ill-treated her, consented to bare her youth and beauty to twenty thousand lustful eyes, and to become a lure round which all that was vicious and prurient in the city began to crawl and gape and gloat. And through all this I had the choice of life or death, and I chose life—through all this!"

"You are exciting yourself most unreasonably. Listen to——"

"I will not; I will speak! It sickened me at first, but I have abased myself into delighting in it. I am the darling of the Greens now. They are generous; they have forgiven me my parentage; they will not visit my father's sins upon me. I am their treasure, their boast, their Godsend; my name is always on their foul lips, my shame is their inexhaustible satisfaction! From all this I warn you back. Leave me! While I am capable of speaking to you thus. Leave me! While you are capable of breaking free; leave me to my vile aptitude for my destiny—before you are bound, life and soul and body, to anything so debased as I am. Leave me! leave me!"

"I will not leave you. Every word you say makes you more precious, more adorable, in my eyes. Your very warning proves to me that you can and will love me—that you love me already. What am I, Ecebolus? Am I so immaculate and squeamish that I am to be scared by the harsh colours in which it is your caprice to paint yourself? I care nothing for your past. I live in the present moment only. I see in you the most beautiful and the most lovable woman on earth, and I will not leave you."

"You are blinded by your passion. You cannot see the abyss on the brink of which you stand—

you, in the prime of your superb youth, with all the world at your feet. You thirst for my beauty and will not reckon the cost of the draught. It is deadly poison ! "

" I care not ; the taste will be that of nectar."

" Wild, reckless, libertine as you are, your follies and excuses are excusable; they spring from impulse and temptation—not from deliberate purpose, like mine. When women like myself take to evil they take to it so mercilessly. But that you cannot understand. The good in you is so much greater than the bad. Your instinct teaches you to refine and purify me. It shows you only what is fair and tempting, not what is hideous and repulsive."

" It teaches me one thing—that you love me— and that is enough for me."

" It deludes you. I cannot love—not even you. The time might come when I should exult in your belonging to me, in my possession of you and dominion over you. Come and stand here—close beside me. So—in front of the mirror. Look at those two—man and woman ; could you find a fairer match? Would you not say that they were made for each other ; that neither could give more than each would receive ; that the woman's perfection would be a fitting supplement to the man, and the man's to the woman ?"

" Now I can agree with you. Then, as fate has brought these two together, so let them remain."

"I will tell you what would happen. The woman's is the stronger nature. The man would be absorbed and lost in her. The triumph and delight he anticipates would be turned into servitude and self-reproach. The rank atmosphere which is congenial to her would be perdition to him ; it would scorch and blight him into a wreck for all that is evil to mock at and exult over, and all that is good to shrink from as from some ideal of iniquity. Leave me ! Let go my hands ! "

"This is raving, Theodora. You must calm yourself, and listen to me. I have at least a right to be heard patiently, for I lay at your feet everything in the world that is mine to give—my life, my fortune, my hand——"

"Madman ! madman ! Let me go ! "

"Not until you have heard me out. It is you who are mad—mad in giving way to this morbid excitement, in thus fighting against your love for me. Do you think I cannot read the meaning of this storm of self-accusation, and these wild predictions of evil to come ? You are battling against the prompting of your own heart, which bids you yield and be mine. You fancy that to yield would be to injure me, and you thus prove your love a hundred times more than if you had consented readily."

"Let me go. And sit down. I am calm now. I

have already told you that I have no love to give
—even to you. My nature is too warped and
embittered to cherish it. I have not even that
sentiment which enables a woman to persuade herself that she can be faithful. I have the curse of
keen appreciation, for in such as I am it becomes a
curse. There is no point in which you are superior
to other men that I do not recognize intensely;
but my recognition is that of passionate caprice,
not of stable affection. I know how you are petted
and idolized by the great world. Is there a matron
in the city so frozen and rigid but she will thaw
and unbend at your address? is there a maiden so
innocent but her pulses will beat the faster at the
bare idea of having you for a suitor? By a word I
can trample on all these puny emotions. I can set
the pearl of price in my coronet of shame, and
flaunt it before all their envious, disappointed eyes.
I can satisfy my own insatiableness, and revenge
myself at a stroke on half society. . . . But I will
not speak that word. I owe you much. Hush!
If I exaggerate my debt to you, it is because I
have met with so little real kindness in my life—
none since I left Hermia's roof. You alone, I
repeat, of all men I have ever met, have not con-
spired for my abasement. You offer me—you—
your life, your fortune, your hand. It is incredible,
absurd!"

"Theodora, I swear to you most solemnly that I

am ready to defy the world and make you my wife."

"God help you! You are hopelessly mad. But listen. If I had to choose this minute between wedlock and crucifixion, I would choose the cross. I might bear the agony, but not the bonds. They would madden me into something worse, if possible, than I am. Now do you see how base I am? Will nothing disgust you with me?"

"Nothing, while I see your love and your better nature shining through all; for you have a better nature, although you persist in repressing it. I have learnt more about you than you imagine. Ask the people at the theatre what is their opinion of you?"

"Ask them! Poor wretches! Because I show them as much consideration as I bestow upon my dog there, they, out of their great thankfulness for small mercies, extol me as a benefactress. Ask them! Do you suppose that a reputation for petty virtues and flimsy amenities can balance the crushing load of turpitude that drags me down; that a relaxation from crime must imply a tendency to innocence? Cannot an assassin be fond of children, or an adulteress doat on birds and flowers? The little good which I do I do from selfish motives, not for its own sake. It cools the fever in my brain and heart, and steadies my nerves. It is a foil to my passions. After the delirium of the theatre it is a relief to mingle with commonplace, practical people, and do commonplace, practical things."

"You are as cruel to yourself as you are to me. But I do not despair. If you will not hear of marriage, make your own terms. You shall feel no other bonds than those which I will weave from day to day—bonds of infinite care and tenderness and devotion—until you own the deliciousness of wearing them ; and then, perhaps, you may begin to wish them permanent. Will you leave Constantinople ? Will you come with me to Tyre ? There I will teach you to forget the past, and to remember only that you are my love, my rescued treasure."

"How gratified your father would be with your Byzantine bride ! "

"He will see only what the mirror showed us— that we are a perfect match—and he will learn to love you for your own sake and mine."

"Ah, heavens ! we must make an end of this. Leave me now, Ecebolus, I entreat you. You will believe that I am grateful ? "

" I must believe you to be only too much so. I shall begin to curse the hour when I was of the least service to you. Had I been like others, without even that paltry claim on you, I might have been more warmly received. You sacrifice me to a fantastic sentiment."

"It hurts you to be refused—you who have

never sued in vain to be refused by me, of all women
on earth. But if you could understand how I long
to kneel before you, to kiss your feet and worship
you in gratitude, you would forgive me. But it is
not love. All through my shameless career I have
cherished a thought of you, as a hero, as something
nobler than other men. Leave me with that thought.
If you are trying to lift me out of the abyss I will
not drag you down into it. You have scarcely
soiled your seraph plumes as yet ; beware lest you
stoop so low that they become clogged with mire,
and you cannot rise again. You have many other
gifts besides your divine beauty. There are times,
I know, when you are ambitious, and aspire to
a loftier career. Foster your ambition. When
you are successful and honoured, when you have
chosen some woman worthy of you, whose heart
is not dead, you will think of me—perhaps less
harshly than others will. You will say, ' She
was vile, but she saved me from herself.' Perhaps,
when you remember all, your blessing even may
mingle with the execrations of a whole city."

" Then why will you not leave the city ? Escape
with me from these expected horrors."

" I cannot give you any reason that you will be
satisfied with. I am under a spell, and must work
out my doom. The other day there was a crowd
at the corner of a street, and my litter was stopped.
I looked out to see what was the matter, and there

were two priests standing close by, one quite young, with a kind, earnest face, the other older and grim-looking. I heard the young man say, 'See, there is Theodora, the dancer. How lovely she is! She looks like an angel of God. Poor girl! And to think that——' But the other interrupted him sternly. What do you think he said? 'Lord, turn away mine eyes, lest they behold iniquity. Call her rather Dæmonodora; she is possessed by seven devils. That woman will corrupt the whole city. She is worse than the plague. That, at least, is the visitation of God, but she is the visitation of hell!'"

"Canting liar!"

"He did not cant or lie. He was a true prophet. I have a mission here; I am impelled to it, and cannot, will not, resist. Sin and shame have been forced upon me; let those who are to blame see to it! They may groan and shudder at the thing I shall become, but they shall also marvel and tremble. I must be Queen of Iniquity and reign supreme. Will you degrade yourself into being my consort? Go, I say—go at once."

"I will go, then, if you desire it so earnestly. When this terrible mood is on you, I am powerless. But I warn you, I will not give you up. I say farewell only for the present. Darling! I cannot leave you so."

"No, no, no! my lips are poison! There, go now—pray go."

And as the door closed behind Ecebolus, the listeners heard one deep, prolonged sigh.

     *   *   *   *   *   *

"Chrysomalla may be sorry to lose you, my pretty dear," soliloquized the ballet-mistress, as she and her companion retreated stealthily from the closet, "but she will not let you cut your own throat if she can help it. He shall learn to find you in your other mood, and then we shall see. You will resist him about as easily as lath and plaster resists Greek fire.—Well, sir, what do you think of her?"

But John meditated, and was silent.

"You had better stay now and have supper," said Chrysomalla. "Suppose we cement our new alliance with a flask of the old Tænaotic. We have plenty to talk over."

CHAPTER XII.

BAITING A TRAP.

As pleasant a spot as any in the city of Constantinople was a terraced slope running parallel to and nearly on a level with a portion of the wall which fronted the harbour, and overshadowed by magnificent chestnut trees. Under their leafy colonnades were many a green nook and sequestered seat, and hither Justinian, who generally rose with the sun, if not before it, was wont to betake himself in the cool of the morning to saunter and meditate, and invigorate his brain with the freshness of the early breeze.

It fell out oddly enough that not long after the events recorded in the preceding chapter, John of Cappadocia was smitten with a similar desire for early rising and matutinal meditation, and consequently one fine morning he and Justinian met face to face under the aforesaid chestnuts.

I have already stated that John had taken

peculiar pains to ingratiate himself with the
nephew of Justin, and had so far succeeded that
the latter began to contemplate with curious
interest the character and fortunes of the Prætorian secretary. It was at once clear to the
intuitive perception of Justinian that John was no
ordinary man, vastly superior to the crowd of
courtiers, idlers, and fops with whom he associated,
and to the general run of secretaries. The mystery
which hung about his origin and antecedents, his
rapid rise from the position of a needy adventurer
to a post of considerable value and importance—
from the status of a man whom everybody was at
first inclined to treat coldly, to one of unmistakable popularity; the unstudied flexibility of his
manner and address, which altogether cancelled
the ungainliness of his person; the breadth and
solidity of his opinions and his free expression of
them, apparently careless of giving offence, and
yet, by the exercise of some spontaneous tact, never
guilty of doing so,—these and many other points
were all noted and appreciated by Justinian, who
possessed a remarkable gift of forming an accurate
estimate of the capacities of those around him,
and who in such estimate exhibited remarkable
tolerance; regarding any deviation from his own
rigid standard of ethics merely as a variety of the
mask which everything human, male or female,
was, either by deliberate choice or by circumstances,

impelled to adopt. That John was a crafty, dangerous man was as clearly revealed to the insight of
Justinian as that he was an able one ; but as became
a student of not impossible empire, the universal
theorist surveyed such a character as an expert
in arms surveys a keen, supple blade, with the
consciousness that in master hands the weapon
becomes a safeguard, the danger being all for those
against whom its keenness and suppleness are
directed.

But on this occasion, as the portly form of the
Cappadocian sauntered towards him, Justinian was
in no affable humour ; for late the previous night
the news had come that the ex-Patriarch Macedonius was lying dead at Gangra, in Galatia, whither
he had fled from Euchaita before an incursion of
Huns ; and from the details of the intelligence it
was clear—to an orthodox mind, at least—that his
death had been compassed by the machinations of
the heretical party, even if the Emperor Anastasius
himself was not personally implicated in the affair,
as there was strong reason to suspect.

The proud, indomitable spirit of the Patriarch
had never been broken by his long, harassed exile,
and his periodical letters to the faithful, which all
the precautions of the Imperialists had failed in
intercepting or suppressing, kept the memory of
his wrongs and his cause before the eyes of
Christendom not less effectually than did the

warlike demonstration of Vitalian, count of the Gothic Federates.

But now it was all over. The indignant beatings of the steadfast heart were stilled for ever, and the restless years of exile merged in the infinite repose of eternity. An incubus was lifted from the souls of the Imperial party, and in the eyes of all the orthodox and the serious-minded and earnest-hearted of the Blue Faction, a new martyr was added to the glorious list of those who had suffered for conscience' sake.

On the receipt of the news Justinian was agitated by various emotions. He had a personal acquaintance with the deceased Patriarch, and professed complete adherence to his rigid Catholicism. He reflected, besides, on the important political bearing of the matter. It was inevitable that the zeal of Vitalian would be again stimulated into activity by the orthodox rendering of Macedonius's last moments. He would recommence the war not only as the champion of Catholicism, but also as the avenger of blood. Should he succeed in entering Constantinople in arms and in deposing Anastasius, he would be irresistible; and, supposing him to decline the purple himself, his selection of a candidate final. Whom would he select? On the other hand, if the Emperor, whose military and naval resources were now thoroughly reorganized, should be victorious, the empire would be secured to his family almost beyond the possibility of opposition. No success is for the time so popular as military success, and an opportune victory covers a multitude of sins. Moreover, the ravages of Vitalian's semi-barbarian army, inflicted periodically year after year, and accompanied by indiscriminate slaughter, had become intolerable to the mass of the inhabitants, and to rid them of this scourge would be to establish the most stringent claim on their gratitude. The religious convictions of men must be indeed strong before they can regard with equanimity wasted lands and murdered relatives, by consoling themselves with the reflection that the author of their desolation is also the champion of their creed.

No one was better able to guess with what anxious interest the news from Gangra must be regarded by Justinian than John of Cappadocia, and in selecting the morning after the arrival of that news for an interview with him on a wholly different and comparatively trivial subject, John might at first sight be accused of clumsy injudiciousness—selecting, because throughout the complexities of his career the element of pure chance played as subordinate a part in the Cappadocian's concerns as it well could in those of any mortal being. A man who could say, " I went to such and such a place on the mere chance of meeting so and so," would be set down as half a simpleton. John was never clumsy or injudicious : he was about to

submit to the most crucial and final test the great
Justiniano-Theodora theory. He was about to
probe Justinian. "If," he argued, "at a time like
the present, when his mind must necessarily be
pre-occupied by matters of vital importance, when,
if ever, his thoughts must be dwelling on his
chances of failure or success in life, Justinian
can be induced to betray an undue interest—ay,
or any interest whatever—in such a woman as
Theodora, my conclusions are correct; I hold in
my hand a secret worth knowing, to whatever end
I may choose to apply the knowledge. Were he
like other men my discovery would be scarcely
worthless; being such as he is, it becomes a
valuable instrument by which to gauge the whole
man. If, on the contrary——"

But there is no need for us to follow the Cappadocian any further in his meditations. Nor shall
we, knowing as much as we do know, derive either
profit or information by listening to the bulk of a
prolonged colloquy carried on between two experts,
both of whom recognized the great principle which
has since their days been so tersely enunciated,
that "language was given us to conceal our
thoughts," either of whom, with a consciousness of
mutual insincerity, felt in his heart an admiration
for the easy reticence and glib dissimulation of the
other.

They were not inclined to dwell too long on a

topic of which it was impossible to avoid all mention, the death of Macedonius. It was delicate
ground for both. But in handling the matter John
had a decided advantage. His practical connection
with it was a thing of the past, and unsuspected
by his companion. The anxieties of Justinian were
prospective, and he was aware that during the present crisis his every word and action would be carefully noted and interpreted—or misinterpreted, as
the case might be—not only by John, but by half
the people in Constantinople.

Gradually, however, as they touched upon subjects less disagreeable and necessitating less caution
in their discussion, the severity and reserve of
Justinian's manner wore off, and he was perhaps
entirely off his guard when John exclaimed with
hearty abruptness—

"As I live, the sun is already high. What is
there like pleasant company to make one forget
how time flies? Your condescension will pardon
an overworked secretary for forcing himself away
somewhat unceremoniously. I must be at the desk
earlier than usual this morning; the work on hand
is enormous. I have not breakfasted, and I have
unwisely pledged myself to executing a small commission in the Agora. As it is, I fear the breakfast
must be deferred." And John sighed, like a man
to whom it was by no means an unimportant matter
to lose his breakfast.

Justinian, who had already earned among the Byzantines the nickname of "the Faster," which clung to him through life, smiled with an air of indulgent superiority. It tickled his peculiar vein of self-appreciation to find a man of the Cappadocian's calibre beset by those petty weaknesses of the flesh, to the attacks of which he himself by temperament and discipline was all but impregnable.

The smile was not lost upon John.

"We are not all, sir," he said, "so happily constituted as yourself, who are able to keep the fire burning day and night, and require but little fuel to replenish it. My gross nature, at least, hankers after material sustenance."

"Perhaps I am more to be pitied than congratulated," said Justinian, blandly. "They tell me I lose a great deal by my insensibility to the good things of this life. Such matters are merely constitutional, and as such trivial. I shrink from seeming officious," he added courteously, "but is the small commission of such importance that it cannot be executed by proxy? It would give me much pleasure to take upon myself the responsibility, and relieve you. I shall be passing through the Agora before noon."

John hesitated, and laughed with a clever pretence of slight embarrassment as he answered. "A thousand thanks for the offer. I am not sure that it is consistent with the dignity of a Prætorian secretary to own to such a commission, or that I can with any

conscience allow the Admirable Justinian to undertake it."

"Can it be so very compromising?" asked
Justinian pleasantly, and making up his mind to
prove that the strictest precisian can relax on
occasion.

"Shall I confess? I promised a fair lady, an
old client of mine, who is confined to the house—
no other than Chrysomalla, the ballet-mistress—to
leave a bracelet, which requires mending, at
Alexander the jeweller's."

Justinian laughed outright—a rare thing with
him. "I have often heard the lady spoken of," he
said, "as a public benefactress, and I am aware
that a lawyer must necessarily keep up an extensive
range of acquaintances. Pray don't apologize for
your own good nature, or exaggerate my notorious
moroseness. I shall be happy, if you will trust
me, to execute your very innocent commission. Is
there any message?"

"My instructions," said John, "were simply to
leave the bracelet. I conclude Alexander will
know what to do with it. Still, it might be as well
to inquire. But do you seriously mean, sir, to be
so gracious?"

"I seriously mean to resuscitate your hopes of
breakfast, if you will permit me."

"And earn my eternal gratitude. It would be
churlish to refuse your kind offer. Here is the

bracelet," continued John, producing a small packet, which he began to unfold. "It is a pretty bauble, but unluckily a stone is missing."

"It is; the gold-work seems fine," said Justinian, with a careless glance at the bracelet. "If that large cavity was filled by a gem of any kind, it must have been of considerable value. Does your fair client think of replacing it?"

"I believe it was an emerald," said John.

Justinian manifested a feeble interest. "The stage must be a lucrative profession," he remarked quietly.

"In some cases it is. The truth is, that although I received the bracelet from Chrysomalla, it does not belong to her. She is merely an agent. The real owner is a much more celebrated lady—Theodora, the dancer."

The closest observer could not have detected any trace of significance in John's look or accent as he spoke. He was to all appearance occupied in minutely examining the chasing of the bracelet; but the senses of the tiger, watching for his victim on the jungle edge, are not more keenly alert than were the Cappadocian's at that instant.

"Theodora!" exclaimed Justinian, with eagerness; and then he stopped short and audibly gulped down the rest of his surprise before it found utterance. In a few seconds a bright tinge of colour spread over his countenance. It was scarcely a blush, but the result of that strong, sudden effort of repression.

The Cappadocian gave one glance at his companion and was satisfied. Then he occupied himself in re-enfolding the bracelet in its various wrappings, as Justinian continued—his voice and manner as calm as ever—"That is, indeed, a different matter. I cease to wonder, but I own to a slight, perhaps improper, curiosity as to who was the victim. Not that I can expect it to be satisfied, but being the bearer——"

"There is no victim in the case," interrupted John, looking up, and with adroit seizure of opportunity transferring the parcel to Justinian's passive hand, "unless it be the dancer herself; otherwise I should not have acccepted your kind offer, or, indeed, undertaken the commission at all."

The scruple and the sentiment had a false ring to Justinian's ears. His good humour and affability began to vanish. He had a sudden suspicion of being overreached. But John proceeded quietly to tell him as much of the story as suited his own purpose.

"She must be a strange girl," said Justinian. What immense force of character she has! I wonder what is the ground of her obligation to Alexander?"

"Money, no doubt. What a sensible, practical

man the Greek is! Of course he might choose his own method of repayment, and—make a fool of himself."

Justinian drew in his breath sharply, and frowned like a man who winces under a sudden pain.

"Ah! it is a miserable affair altogether. To look at what she is, and to think what she might have been, with a happier fate!"

"And still may be," added John, sententiously.

"It is too late," said Justinian, in his deepest, gravest tones.

"I doubt if it is ever too late," returned John, cheerfully, without the least intention of uttering a Christian sentiment. "But I know who will be. You will now permit me, sir, to thank you again for your great courtesy and consideration, and to take my leave." And he bowed himself off, leaving Justinian standing under the trees with Theodora's bracelet in his hand. "I got away just in time," muttered the arch-schemer, as he hailed a litter outside the gardens; "in another minute he would have retracted his offer. In ten minutes he will hate me. Never mind; let the poison work for a few days, and then to sound Alexander. He owes me a good turn for getting him out of that pawn-broking scrape and introducing him to Ecebolus. One cannot have too many irons in the fire. And now for breakfast." And when John, who had

ample time to spare, reached home, he was capable
of dismissing all business from his mind, and
settling down to his meal with the thorough
sensual enjoyment of a greedy child.

But Justinian remained for some time longer in
the retirement of the walks, pondering on the
strange issue of his meeting with the Cappadocian.
He found it difficult to account for the deep anxiety
and irritation which it had produced. Excepting
by the one exclamation, which could not possibly
have been intelligible in its full import to the
perspicacity of any human being, he could not
accuse himself of having, in the remotest degree,
betrayed the dormant secret which the sound of
Theodora's name had roused into sudden life.
Nevertheless, he was oppressed by an intolerable
sense of uneasiness and alarm. He could not help
feeling like a detected man. The concatenation of
incidents was too strange. That he, cherishing a
sentiment to which of all men on earth he should
be most callous, should suddenly find himself in a
position painfully coincident with that sentiment!
That the offer which he had made in mere courtesy
should result in so fantastic an incongruity!
Justinian, the strictest disciplinarian in Constantinople, acting as middle-man between a notorious
wanton and her jeweller! The offer had certainly
come spontaneously from himself, and in a natural
sequence of conversation, and yet he could not

shake off the notion that the Cappadocian had
inveigled him into the difficulty, and taken his
departure without giving him time to reflect and
change his mind.

We know that Justinian's suspicions were perfectly correct, and if we are inclined to think that
his morbid sensitiveness was making a mountain
of a molehill, that it mattered little whether the
bracelet was Theodora's or Chrysomalla's, and that
by the exercise of a minimum of plain sense he
might have treated the affair as a jest—possibly in
bad taste, but still a jest—have simply executed
the commission he had been rash enough to undertake, and even amused himself with picturing the
tacit surprise of that discreetest of men, Alexander,
at the channel through which his bracelet came
back to him, let us remember that the sting of the
whole occurrence was its terrible consistence with
the truth. There was no real incongruity. The
bracelet in his hand was an actual symbol of the
thought which soiled his mind. It accused him
like a living witness, and its accusation was un-
answerable. He might cast it from him, but he
could not pluck out of his brain the idea which it
typified. Let us remember his pride in his own
moral strength, in his abnegation of those natural
impulses to which most men yielded, and his
contempt for and horror of all such weakness and
incontinence; the tortures of self-reproach and

agonies of shame he had undergone as he felt the fatal fancy which possessed him gaining ground daily; how he had struggled and wrestled and prayed against the insidious temptation, and in the midst of his prayers, his study, his fasting and penance, it was still there, tempting him like the fair fiend who tempted St. Anthony. But lately at least he believed himself to have gained the mastery, and to be fortified against further attacks. He had almost recovered his old self-confidence. Why, only a few minutes before, he had felt a pitying surprise at John's blunt confession that the postponement of a meal was to him a matter for regret, and had secretly applauded himself for being superior to such petty frailties; and now, by what a sudden, bitter blow was that momentary self-complacency avenged! What were a hundred frailties in a man like John of Cappadocia, who made no pretence of being better than his neighbours, to the one deadly backsliding in Justinian? How utterly futile and worthless must be his powers of resolve, when the mention of a harlot's name, and the touch of a bauble belonging to her, could send a thrill through every fibre of his being!

Before noon Justinian visited the shop of Alexander, at that time all but deserted. In the afternoon it usually presented a very different appearance, when the fashionable ladies and male exquisites dropped in by scores, some few to make purchases, the majority to lounge, flirt, talk scandal, and look over jewellery, for the simple pleasure of handling and criticizing the costly gems.

Alexander was a great and useful man in his line, blending with considerable talent the professions of banker, money-lender, scandal-monger, goldsmith, jeweller, and dealer in works of art generally. But although for the benefit of his fair patrons he had all the gossip of Constantinople at the tip of his tongue, he was never known to make a blunder or offend any one. It was well understood that a more discreet or safer man was never entrusted with important secrets; which was perhaps as well, for the splendour of many a gorgeous insect of either sex which fluttered in the glare of the Byzantine Court was dependent on the accommodating generosity of Alexander, and in the keeping of his strong boxes lay the credit of many a noble family. However unrelenting he might be to his victims of an inferior class, the cunning Greek dealt leniently with the upper ranks of society, and was careful not to damage his business by bringing matters to an unpleasant crisis in their case. Once only, and that at the beginning of his career, had he got himself into a difficulty, and then the ingenuity and hardihood of his counsel, John of Cappadocia, rescued him from imminent danger. The lesson was not thrown away, and Alexander was now the wealthiest and most popular man of his class in the city. He was especially indulgent to the fair sex, and, if report spoke truly, had no aversion to the personal security of a pretty face, and a pair of beseeching eyes.

Very rarely did Justinian enter the shop; as a rule only when his opinion was requested on the merits of a new design, or the genuineness of some art treasure. Now, therefore, when Alexander saw the grave countenance of the man of the future on his threshold, alone and at this unwonted hour, he had an instantaneous perception of something remarkable, and came forward himself with obsequious haste to receive his visitor.

"Your Condescension overwhelms me with favour," said the Greek, with a low obeisance. "In what can I have the honour of being of service to your Nobility?"

Before answering, Justinian involuntarily glanced round him. There were but two or three people in the shop besides the assistant, and they were intent upon their own affairs. He never thought of looking back into the glare of the Agora, where, besides his own parasol-bearer, two men at some little distance from each other were basking idly in the sunshine nearly opposite the entrance of Alexander's shop.

The quick-witted Greek interpreted the glance. "I shall esteem it a great favour," he said, "if your Excellence will deign to step into my private chamber. I have just received an antique vase from Persia, golden and of incomparable workmanship, on which I humbly solicit your unerring judgment."

Justinian acquiesced with a bow, and Alexander ushered him through an inner shop into a large apartment, exquisitely furnished and overlooking a quiet garden. The window was secured by a network of strong bars, and a glimpse of the visible contents of the room suggested that the precaution was not superfluous. Disposed in cabinets round the walls, or exhibited on slabs and tables of costly marbles, of delicate mosaic and rare woods, was a collection of objects of either great intrinsic value, rarity, or matchless workmanship, gathered from every clime under the sun. Gems, plate, enamels, bronzes, ivories, arms, statuary; and each article a perfect specimen of its kind. Nothing commonplace found its way into Alexander's inner chamber.

But when once inside, and the door closed behind them, the merchant knew his business too well to press an immediate inspection of his treasures, but waited quietly for Justinian to begin, which he did at once.

" I have undertaken a commission—to deliver this bracelet to you; it is your own manufacture, I believe, and has to be repaired." And Justinian handed the packet to the jeweller.

At the sight of the bracelet, whatever surprise Alexander may have felt, he manifested none.

"Ah! I see the stone is missing," he said, simply. "Is it lost?"

"I have been told so," replied Justinian. "But I know little about it."

"It is a thousand pities," said Alexander. "It was a Scythian emerald without flaw, and of peculiar shape. I have at this moment no cut stone of the same sort which can fill its place in the setting. But if time is not an object——"

"I really cannot give you any information on that point," said Justinian, coldly; "indeed, I am quite ignorant of, and have no interest in, the matter. Have you no instructions what is to be done to the bracelet?"

"I have received none." Alexander began to be rather perplexed. There was a short pause, and then he said, with some slight hesitation, "You are possibly aware, Noble sir, to whom the bracelet was supplied?"

"To Theodora, the dancer," answered Justinian, steadily. "I have also been informed that the stone was lost in the theatre, and has not been found."

"Your Nobility will permit me to suspect," said Alexander, with a smile, "that some one has found it. It may yet be recovered. I could swear to the stone among ten thousand."

"I dare say you are right. It does not, however, concern me. I have fulfilled my part and delivered the bracelet. In due time you will probably receive your instructions."

Alexander was unlocking a drawer in a small cabinet. He had great experience in certain phases of human nature. Strange to say, the evident desire of Justinian to repudiate all connection with the bracelet rendered him bolder.

"Permit me, sir," he said, selecting a stone from a number in the drawer, "to show you this sapphire. See what a depth of colour; the genuine azure of the Propontis, and not the suspicion of a flaw! The shape, too, is nearly identical with that of the lost emerald. This is the only gem in my possession for the moment which, as a jeweller who—forgive my presumption—regards his own credit, I could conscientiously recommend in its place. Let us suppose the sapphire filling the cavity thus, these scales encrusted with diamonds of moderate size, to enhance and yet not detract from the beauty of the central stone, and I verily believe I should have improved on my original design."

Justinian smiled at the professional enthusiasm of the jeweller. "I for one shall not dare to dispute your accurate taste in such matters," he said, courteously.

"Your Condescension flatters me," said Alexan-

der, locking the stone and bracelet into the cabinet
and dropping the subject. "This is the vase of
which I spoke. May I venture to hope that it has
your approbation?"

"It is magnificent!" exclaimed Justinian, in-
specting with unfeigned admiration the massive
vessel of pure gold which the Greek placed before
him. "The execution and relief of the figures is
superb."

"I have seen nothing finer during my experience," said Alexander. "It has a long and curious
history, and was once in the possession of the
royal line of Persia; but the work is undoubtedly
that of a Greek artist of the best period."

"It is worthy both of your country and the
Great King," said Justinian.

As he continued his examination of the vase,
Alexander began to gossip.

"There is a sad piece of news from Sycæ this
morning, Noble sir."

"And that is—— ? "

"That his Respectability Malchus expired last
night in a fit, consequent on the discovery of his
wife's infidelity."

"Wretched man!" exclaimed Justinian. "It
is a just retribution for his duplicity and cruelty to
his unfortunate nephew."

"For that, sir—I have it on the best private
authority—he has made late amends. He has

long been suspicious of the Lady Vivia, and when his will is published it will be found that he has left all his large fortune to young Sittas."

"Who is now a rebel and in arms against his Emperor," said Justinian. "Much good it will do him, poor lad."

"May we not trust, sir, that, considering his very peculiar and hard case, he may still be pardoned if he throw himself on the clemency of Cæsar?"

"There is often a difficulty in pardoning rebels with large fortunes," said Justinian, dryly. "And as in all probability war is again imminent—— " But here he checked himself, and an expression of gloomy severity settled on his countenance.

"Ah, that noble martyr and saint!" exclaimed Alexander, softly. "I have one relic which I shall now treasure beyond everything in my possession. This belonged to his sainted Holiness;" and the jeweller opened a case which lay on a table by itself and showed a small golden crucifix ornamented with precious stones. "He had an exquisite taste."

Justinian turned silently away towards the door.

"Shall I inform your Excellence if I receive any instructions regarding the bracelet?" inquired Alexander, as they passed out.

"It is quite unnecessary; if I have any curiosity

on the subject, I can easily satisfy it when I happen to be passing this way."

. "I am always your Nobility's most devoted slave."

And Justinian went his way, with the poison working in his veins.

BOOK III.

CHAPTER I.

SAINT OR SAGE?

THERE could be no doubt that a renewal of the Religious War was inevitable. The aged Emperor seemed to have nearly recovered his health and altogether his obstinacy; he now set the Pope at defiance, and refused to make any concessions whatever.

The preparations for war had been carried on energetically all through the armistice. Within the inner harbour ships were building and refitting day and night. All the engineering skill of the city was incessantly employed in the strengthening of fortifications and the construction of war engines. The arsenal turned out balistas and catapults by the dozen weekly, and according to the chronicles of the times the triumph of science was displayed in a set of gigantic burning glasses, such as Archimedes had used against the fleet of Marcellus during the siege of Syracuse seven centuries before, and by means of which it was intended to set fire to the Gothic vessels from off the ramparts.

Equal care had been bestowed upon the re-organization of the army. The numerical strength of the regiments was increased, and by a judicious system of drafting and redrafting, each levy of recruits was steadied by an admixture of tried veterans.

The use of the modern term " regiment " in this and many a subsequent passage can be justified. The glorious name of legion still existed; but the corps which in the good old times contained ten thousand men, and was an army in itself, now numbered scarce as many hundreds. There is impropriety in bestowing on a dwarf the appellation of a giant.

The landward defence of the city and the guardianship of the Imperial person was entrusted to Justin; Marinus the Syrian, a man of proved courage and experience, being nominated admiral of the fleet.

On the other hand, the armament of Vitalian had to a certain extent deteriorated during the period of inactivity. Either the Count of the Federates was guiltless of those designs on the sovereignty which were imputed to him, and, once more putting faith in the solemn promises of Anastasius that he would comply with the requisitions of the orthodox

party, had permitted a considerable portion of his
army to disband itself, now that the ostensible
object of the war had been obtained; or he was in
reality powerless to detain the wild and independent
warriors who at the first scent of blood and booty
had flocked to him from the Danubian provinces
and the shores of the Euxine Sea, and to whom a
longer sojourn in the wasted and depopulated plains
of Thrace offered but little attraction while the
chance of sharing in the plunder of Constantinople
seemed as remote as ever. But in spite of many
desertions from his standard, he was still encamped
at Anchialus with a formidable force inured to battle
and accustomed to victory. His fleet still lay off
Sycæ, and held the command of the Bosphorus,
and it was certain that the repeated perjury of the
Emperor, and now the death of Macedonius, would
spur him into making every effort for revenge, or,
from another point of view, afford a fresh pretext
for grasping at the purple.

But the new outbreak of the war was yet only
prospective; no overt act of hostility had taken
place on either side.

About this time another of the subordinate
characters in our drama had the happiness to
quit the stage for ever, full of years and good
works—Ariadne the Empress; to the domestic
sorrow and political satisfaction of her husband,
who honoured and possibly loved her as the

authoress of his fortunes, and suffered continual annoyance from what the sentiment of the times will bear me out in terming the intensely cerulean hue of her convictions.

After her obsequies had been celebrated with due pomp, the polluted current of Byzantine life flowed merrily on, as if the tranquillity of the moment was begotten of enduring peace rather than of intermitted war; and on its surface the buzzing swarm of ephemera, bred of corruption and nourished by miasma, danced and fluttered in the delusive radiance.

The Court blazed and strutted and circled in all its peacock magnificence before the mulish octogenarian who was credited with the dominion of the Eastern world; the great dames spent six days in overdressing and undressing, painting and bejewelling themselves, and on the seventh crowded to applaud the declamations of their favourite preachers against the world, the flesh, and the devil, bowing themselves before the lash with a delicious appreciation of the chastisement, and went their way much refreshed to talk scandal and meditate intrigue.

The gilded youth sat down to eat and rose up to play, its languid interest far more excited by a trial between thoroughbreds, and by speculations on the chances of Blue and Green at the next races, than by the movement and machinations of Goth, Emperor, or Pope.

The common herd toiled and sweated and groaned, cursing alike all powers and dominions, spiritual and temporal, and consoling themselves, like their betters, with visions of feasts and spectacles to come. What matter who provided them so long as they were provided ?

And of the personages of our tale each one went on doing with all his or her might whatever their hands had found to do, either for good or evil.

Juliana Patricia encouraged the orthodox, extolled the Council of Chalcedon, and attended to her schools and charities; Maria looked after her handmaidens, and her husband, whom no one now had the least desire to sever from her fond embrace. He had proved himself unequal to command, and was henceforth reserved for the faint chance of being at some future day capable of government.

Ecebolus and Paris devoted themselves to their respective loves; Demas trained his horses and Chrysomalla her girls, and week after week a hundred thousand eager eyes did base homage before the white, glancing feet of Theodora.

But to one person at least in Constantinople the rumours of war came like good tidings of great joy—to our young hero, Belisarius. The martial instinct of his Thracian ancestors awoke within him as he smelt the battle afar off. He burned to distinguish himself in the field, and there appeared a fair chance of his having at all events the opportunity of so doing.

For Justinian, who, when it suited his fancy and there was no reason for suspicion or jealousy, could be a kind and considerate patron, had noticed the young man's melancholy and distraction, so inconsistent with his years and appearance, and, by dint of patient questioning, induced Belisarius to open his heart and make a sufficiently full confession of his present sorrows and disappointments, and his longings for the future. It was clear that the Thracian's natural bent was all towards military service, and that, although he discharged his household duties with the same zeal and fidelity he would have displayed in any duty, they were utterly irksome and distasteful to him; therefore Justinian, with some wonder and vexation at the boy's choice, undertook to obtain from his uncle Justin a promise that, failing a vacancy in the general's own body-guard, the name of Belisarius should be forthwith placed on the roll of one of the cavalry regiments. It is scarcely needful to say that the promise was readily given by the veteran, who at this precise moment would have been only too glad to secure the services of several thousand recruits of the same calibre as the splendid young Thracian.

The latter had never set eyes upon Antonina since the day when they parted by the water-side, and with the strong, simple sense of the right which was one of his chief characteristics, he resolved to avoid meeting her, if possible, until she was safely the wife of Paris. It had been settled that the marriage should shortly take place. Then, indeed, she would be too great a lady to bestow a thought upon a mere trooper in a cavalry regiment. But how if he could succeed in doing something to make himself famous ? Ah ! then it would be all too late. It must be confessed that these reflections did not bring much balm to the bosom of Belisarius, and we need not pursue them.

In the mean time, by the pouting damsels of Justinian's household, who in vain whispered and giggled, and cast languishing glances from the casements of the women's quarter, or devised pretty stratagems for throwing themselves in the way of the handsome stranger, he was accounted a young man of singular insensibility and want of appreciation.

The day after Justinian had visited the shop of Alexander a message was delivered to the latter in the name of Theodora, to the effect that she could not afford to treat herself to another emerald to replace the lost one, and that the jeweller was welcome to do what he pleased with the bracelet, and could credit her with the value of the gold in any future purchase.

On receipt of this message the sagacious Greek

thought fit, for reasons best known to himself, to accept its authority without further reference to the actress herself, and moreover to forget the last words of Justinian as he left the shop. The same evening, seeing one of the household crossing the Agora, he had the audacity to entrust to him a letter for his master.

The first impulse of the usually temperate Justinian on casting his eye over the missive was to vent unreasonable wrath on the head of the meek slave who delivered it. But his habitual self-control asserted itself, and he contented himself by tearing the letter into fragments. Then in due time he became ashamed of his own petulance in being vexed even for an instant at the importunity of a presumptuous tradesman, who was after all but obeying his instinct in never throwing away a chance of custom.

Before long he was able to reflect, with indulgent complacency, on the supposition of Alexander that he had an interest in the concerns of Theodora.

Finally, although he was himself as yet unconscious of the fact and would have fiercely repudiated the idea, a consciousness of the possibility that two other persons had a suspicion of the shameful secret over which he had brooded so long, and might regard it without consternation, produced a sense of positive relief.

Human nature is vain and weak even at its best,

and the sequence of debasing thought easy when it coincides with inclination. Nevertheless, these apparently mean and pitiful sentiments were not the sign of a rapid and complete demoralization, but simply of a reaction, more healthy than otherwise. They led Justinian into forming a remarkable resolution, which, if it did not effect his complete cure, was at least the means of bringing about a radical change, and of relieving his mind from the paralyzing depression under which it was labouring.

A long process has been condensed into a few paragraphs. In tracing the change a digression may be permitted.

We have all of us heard somewhat of the heroic cowardice of those holy men of old, who, feeling themselves unequal to converting the world in which they lived, or impotent to resist its manifold allurements, fled to the solitude of the desert or the cell of the Laura, and devoted the remainder of their lives to the less arduous task of sustaining a personal conflict with the powers of darkness.

The sixth century was prodigal of these champions. At the date of this chapter there were living men who could remember having seen in the flesh St. Simeon the elder, "the most holy and aerial martyr," bowing on his pillar sixty feet high, which he never quitted during thirty years! There were born children who might be gratified one day by the sight of his imitator, St. Simeon the younger, in a similar state of bodily and mental exaltation; and the intervening period was adorned by the revelation of a host of stars of lesser magnitude, from whom may be selected a third Simeon, of Emessa, as a type of another class of saints who, having passed through the ordeal of their seclusion and attained the requisite pitch of virtue, were enabled to partially renew their acquaintance with mankind and perform wondrous works; and also because the historical record of his conduct illustrates so strikingly the state of religious feeling at that time.

We cannot do better than listen to the graphic words of the chronicler, a practical advocate of Antioch.

"Simeon was a man who had so completely divested himself of all vainglory so as to appear insane to those who did not know him, although filled with wisdom and divine grace. He lived chiefly in retirement, and revealed to no one his method of propitiating God, or his seasons for fasting and eating. In the public thoroughfares he frequently appeared to lose his self-control, and to become entirely bereft of reason and discretion. At such times he would enter the first tavern and satisfy his hunger with whatever food he could lay hands on, but if any one saluted him he would depart in anger and haste, as if jealous that his especial merits should be recognized. Such was his conduct in public, but with some of his intimates he was on terms of undisguised familiarity."

We can but glance at the further statement that this good but eccentric man was twice accused by the unrighteous of yielding to the sweet temptation against which St. Anthony was proof, and that by the testimony of the supposed partner of his frailty he was able to refute the atrocious calumny. He performed many miracles.

But these men were among the shining lights of saint-errantry, and of such, who battled to the end against incarnate Pandemonium and died triumphant, we have records enough and to spare. But what of the rank and file who passed and left no sign ?

We have records of these also, the more significant for their comprehensive vagueness. We know that thousands were crushed by the ghastly strife into brutish and ferocious callousness, that numbers were driven into madness or suicide. These latter were no doubt the more passionate and subtle natures, whose organism was too delicate to withstand the assaults of their imagination. Could we learn the details of such cases we should probably discover that they were also among those who most persistently shunned all communion with their kind, who from shame or pride struggled with their temptations in utter loneliness, rejecting all earthly sympathy, and blotting out their glimpses of heaven by the lurid vapours they evoked from hell.

An opportune contact with the world they
avoided might have rescued these unfortunates
from their dismal fate. At the terrible moment
when the fatal crisis was at hand, when the tense
cord was about to snap and the black abyss of
despair, yawned for its victim, a word of blunt
advice, of harsh rebuke, or coarse sarcasm—the
blunter, the harsher, the coarser the more efficacious—might have averted the catastrophe.

The peasants of the East, when passing at night
through a forest said to be haunted, shout and sing
under pretence of scaring away the demons. They
do this, in reality, to encourage each other by neu-
tralizing the oppresive influence of the silent gloom.
The commonest sounds connected with human
interest, a distant laugh, a holloa, the tinkle of a
bell, have been known to save men whose reason
was tottering from ghostly terrors. The most
obstinate apparition will vanish before the whistle
of a belated ploughboy, or the crack of a carter's
whip. A floating twig, sear and leafless, may
rouse the castaway drifting on the desolate sea
from the listlessness of incipient insanity, and
make him take to the oars again with fresh hope.

These are but trivial illustrations, but they may
serve their purpose. Justinian was no recluse, nor
altogether an ascetic. He was a talented, accomplished, and urbane man, with an excellent taste
and a keen perception of the beautiful in art and

nature ; but his organization was bifold, and in one half of it he was as much isolated by thought and habit from the society which surrounded him as if he had been the fanatical tenant of a den in the wilderness. He was superstitious, as were most people in those days, and very religious, as were many, with that kind of religion which shows the greatest outward reverence for all things sacred, is constant in its devotions, public and private, regular in its charities, and is never known to do anything wrong and frivolous ; but the Christian virtues which he most affected were those which he held to be the most consistent with the aspirations of a student and philosopher *in esse*, and a ruler of men *in posse*, and likely to assist in preserving the intellect serene and the body in healthy subjection. These were exactly the virtues in which Byzantine society did not excel; therefore, despising his neighbours, he had modelled himself on the pattern of the monkish fanaticism which taught—and still does teach—human creatures to ignore their humanity, and to account as abominable and alien the faintest symptoms of the yearnings which were implanted in the flesh by the same Power which created it. Under the microscopic self-examination of such a creed essential weaknesses are magnified into portentous sins, unnatural prominence is given to natural impurities, as under the lens an innocent drop of water becomes peopled with terrific shapes.

After some years of excessive abstinence and self-repression, Justinian believed himself, and was believed by others, to be as secure from vulgar desires and cravings as St. Simeon on his pillar. His nature was, indeed, incapable of nourishing an altogether gross affection. Had he been a shade less earnest, the specious argument was fairly open to him that his passion for Theodora sprang into sudden existence through her appearance and conduct at the Cynegium, when she was guiltless of all but misfortune, and was based upon far higher grounds than mere animal impulse. It is, perhaps, to his credit that he rejected this plea of extenuating circumstances, and rebuked the insidious whisper by the stern comment that a pure affection cannot or ought not to survive the utter degradation of its object. A grand but erroneous theory. Justinian then, having suddenly discovered himself to be human, began to fancy himself diabolical. There is always an unwholesome fascination about monstrosities, whether ideal or actual. A placid tolerance of our own frailties may be dangerous, but a hideous exaggeration of them is doubly so. The result is an idolatry of self-mortification : the soul grovels, and is crushed beneath a Juggernaut of its own raising. The emotion which was excited within Justinian at the sight of Theodora was probably felt in various phases by scores of honest, commonplace citizens who made light of it as natural, and consequently got the better of it with comparative ease. Even for those inexcusable sensualists who indulged it without scruple, it lost its charm as it became familiar. But to him as he battled with it the thought assumed the proportions of a gigantic evil, an Antæus-like iniquity, which rose against him with fresh strength each time that he smote it to earth.

If we concede the point that he was incapable of descending to deliberate animalism, there were sufficient grounds for his horror and alarm. Consider who he was and who she was, and the vast gulf which lay between them. He was a man whom the veriest scoffer and libertine in the city had long since ceased to ridicule for his extreme notions, had come to regard as all but infallible. It seemed scarcely more impossible that the grand effigy of Joshua commanding the sun to stay its course should descend from its pedestal in the Forum and commence a flirtation with the awful serenity of the colossal Pallas, than that Justinian should be guilty of any deviation from the strictest propriety.

And she—if my readers have not misunderstood me, in what words can I intensify the simple statement, that she was Theodora, the dancer ? Between such a pair what connecting link was possible, except one of hideous shame and degradation ?

Consider the fearful strain of the double part which Justinian was obliged to play.

As has been said, in one half of his dividuality he was a man of the world, and met the world face to face; in the other, he was an austere fanatic, and shrunk from its fellowship. The recluse who fled into the wilderness confessed his weakness by the very act, and was credited with passions and temptations. If he thought fit to struggle with them in complete seclusion, that was his concern; it was open to, and optional with him, to seek human advice and consolation. If he triumphed, he was adored as a saint; if he succumbed in the struggle, he was pitied.

Justinian had established himself to be without passions and superior to weakness. He had set himself on a pedestal above his fellows, and lacked courage to cast himself down. Such self-iconoclasm was beyond him. He did not dare to admit *his* world into *his* solitude, to disclose to it his frailty, and to ask its aid or sympathy in his temptation. The lines of his dual existence ran parallel, and could never meet without ruin and confusion. Every finger would be pointed and every tongue loosed in scorn of the man who had aspired so high and fallen so low. No; he must wrestle to the end alone. In the nocturnal solitude of his chamber he might grovel in a paroxysm of shame and self-condemnation, but he must meet the world by day with the lofty attitude of a blameless man.

In spite of a certain degree of constitutional

nervousness in the presence of material danger, to
which allusion has already been made, Justinian
was strong in mind as well as body. He girded
up his loins for the fight and went in boldly against
his temptation, smiting it hip and thigh with all the
weapons of spiritual warfare—penance, fasting, and
supplications; but his prayers were character-
istically rather for power to conceal than for strength
to overcome, less for humility than to escape being
humbled. After repeated encounters his ultimate
victory seemed secure. The hydra with which he
battled lay, to all appearance, crushed and lifeless.
Then suddenly, at the sight and touch of that
accursed gold, it revived, and began to writhe and
struggle fiercely.

And out of this at last came relief. A light broke
upon Justinian. Not the divine beam which en-
lightens the soul of the purified sinner who has
passed through the ordeal and emerged a saint,
but a ray from the earthly torch of human reason
and practical sense, piercing the gloom of fanatical
despondency.

From the moment when his first irritation at the
receipt of Alexander's letter subsided, the reaction
set in. His mind cleared. He found himself able
to argue the question dispassionately, without becoming involved in a whirl of extravagant emotion.
He would consider the matter from the very first.
He would trace the progress of his passion through

all its past phases, and reflect temperately on its probable duration. What was the real origin and nature of this irresistible attraction of Justinian, the student of empire, towards a dancer?—an attraction of which a Greek jeweller and a Cappadocian adventurer—for of John's complicity in the matter he had persuaded himself—could at once conceive the possibility, and of which he himself could not think without a shudder of horror. He would arraign the phantasy at the judgment-seat of pure reason, unbiassed by the antagonism of prejudice or principle, social or religious. He meditated nothing foul or debasing—of that he felt sure; nothing unworthy of a Christian and a philosopher. Even at the theatre on the day of the wedding, when the perfection of her young beauty and grace had first been revealed to him, his appreciation of the artist was marred by his pity for the woman; he had not been conscious of any grosser feeling.

Justinian was a man of mature years and great acquirements, but in all that concerned woman and womanly influences he was as much a novice as Belisarius. And in this wise he entered upon the third stage of a passion which, like that of the young Thracian, was destined to be his solitary one and to last through life. Its sudden conception had filled him with contemptuous surprise. Its progress, in spite of his opposition, had terrified him—it is impossible to speak of him without recognition of his duality; the new phase of philosophic review and analysis brought with it a delicious calm, like that of the ocean still heaving with the memory of the tempest, but capable of reflecting from a tranquil surface the grateful sunshine and the blue of heaven. The last stage was yet to come, but not until time had brought many a strange vicissitude to all in whom we may have conceived an interest. In most people it is a dangerous symptom when they begin to reason about that from which at first they instinctively shrank, but Justinian must not be judged by a common standard. His present condition was on all counts safer than his last. Great vehemence of feeling is liable to violent revulsion, and the rabid saint of to-day may be the reckless sinner of to-morrow.

When Justinian resolved to dismiss from his mind all prejudices and preconceptions likely to interfere with the exercise of pure reason, which he proposed to himself in the analysis of his passion, there remained the element of superstition, which it was impossible for him to get rid of. It was part of his nature, inasmuch as it was common to the nature of all men, high and low, in that age. This was so far unfortunate, that in his research he was likely to arrive at sundry points where credulity, backed by the phantom of a wish, might succeed in discerning, according to its especial view, the hand either of destiny or of providence. I have spoken before of the superstition of the Byzantines, but to conclude this chapter with a short reconsideration of it will not be amiss.

To begin with, it was tripartite; it might have in it a preponderance of Christian or of heathen sentiment, or it might be compounded of equal parts of both. In one shape or the other it was bound to exist in every one.

Paganism was far from being extinct;—it is not yet extinct in the nineteenth century,—a large proportion of its traditions having been ingeniously dovetailed into and assimilated with the mysteries of Christianity. It would have puzzled a curious investigator to decide whether the old faith or the new predominated in the hybrid creed of a large section of the population. Some years later, indeed, we hear of the discovery, by a zealous bishop, of seventy thousand unmistakable heathens in only four provinces by no means the most remote from the capital, and are told that even the ranks of Byzantine society furnished a tolerable muster of unbelievers. It was consequently a period when ideas of destiny, doom, lucky stars, evil eyes, charms, countercharms, and such like nonsense exercised an important influence even among people of high position and understanding; when such expressions as good luck and bad luck were literally household words. The domestic routine of each day produced a respectable crop of omens, and the trade of prophet and soothsayer flourished like a green bay tree.

The heathen hag Fortune certainly laboured hard to retain the allegiance of her votaries by the splendid instances of her favouritism which she set before them. It seemed only necessary for a man to be born under a lucky star, to have fair abilities and some audacity, and he might rise to be anything. We need not go out of our way for examples ; take the case of the last four Emperors of the East.

Marcian had arrived in Constantinople from Thrace so penniless that he had to borrow a small sum to start upon. Leo had risen to be military steward in the household of Aspar, the great Patrician and ancestor of Vitalian, and was nominated to the purple by his master, who intended to govern through him, in which intention, by the way, he was resolutely frustrated by Leo. Zeno, an Isaurian mountaineer of obscure birth, had married the Princess Ariadne and succeeded to the throne through her. At his death she married again, this time Anastasius, a domestic in the palace, who thus became the present Emperor. Then Justin, the commander of the guards, and uncle of Justinian, was originally a Dacian peasant, and had marched into Constantinople with a knapsack on his back ; he too—but I must not anticipate the fortunes of those whose story I am telling. The rigid ceremonial of the Byzantine court, where the enormous scale of precedence was subdivided with fractional minuteness, and the violation of these nice distinctions punishable as a criminal offence, was curiously co-existent with this tolerance of ignoble birth and doubtful antecedents. Regarding marriage as a means of success, the fair sex had an equal right to aspire, and the prediction of a noble or wealthy suitor brought many a rich fee into the pockets of the fortune-tellers. From that day to this no one has succeeded in inventing a prophecy more grateful to feminine ears.

But the character of Justinian's superstition was essentially Christian. His youth had been watchfully superintended by those two excellent Dacian ladies, his mother Vigilantia and his aunt Lupicina, who were patterns of piety and orthodoxy scarcely inferior to Juliana Patricia himself. Any symptoms of paganism which cropped up here and there in their teaching were as unimportant as the occasional provincialisms which tinged their speech. And here was presented an almost more extensive field for superstition. There were few really religious persons of any standing but believed that they had secured the interest and could depend upon the services of at least several patron saints and martyrs, the deputies and proxies of Providence, to whose interposition they referred most of the ordinary and all the unusual occurrences of life—the only alternative being the very unpleasant one of diabolical agency, which we know that for the present Justinian had abandoned. If these saintly guardians attended to half the petty requirements of their clients, or performed half the menial work with which they were credited, their celestial hands must have been inconveniently full of, and not a little soiled by, earthly business.

Ah, well! our enlightenment may be pardoned a smile at the cumbrous polytheistic Christianity of the Byzantines, but it might be as well if the doctrine of the sparrow's fall sounded a little more significantly in modern ears than it does. One serious caution may not be misplaced. Let us reserve judgment until the end. Theodora, fallen, shameless, degraded, may nevertheless justify her name and prove to be the gift of God; that which man condemns as common and unclean, to be the instrument of Omnipotence.

CHAPTER II.

WHEELS WITHIN WHEELS.

One afternoon, as Belisarius was stretching and yawning on a bench in the court-yard, bored and discontented, and quite regardless of a forward maiden who, under cover of doing needlework by the window for the Lady Lupicina, was making eyes at him with all her gentle might, he received a summons to attend Justinian in his apartments.

On entering the room he noticed at once that his patron was looking paler and more careworn than he had ever seen him. This was particularly striking, because for some time previously Justinian had been in unusual, for him even buoyant, spirits, being at the best but undemonstrative in his emotions.

He was seated at a table on which were writing materials, a letter ready folded, and a small packet. For some moments he regarded the

Thracian fixedly without speaking, and then began in his deep tones—

"Young man, I have reason to believe that as you possess strength and daring far beyond your years, so also you are gifted with singular discretion and self-control. A union of such qualities is not common amongst us; with them you cannot fail to rise in the profession you have chosen, especially as you have begun by learning to obey simply, and to hold your tongue."

Belisarius bowed in acknowledgment of this complimentary preamble, which, not being given to protestation, was about all he could do. Justinian continued—

"I have a special service to entrust to you, the last, possibly, before you leave my household and enter upon your new duties, but you may depend on my never losing sight of those who have given me satisfaction. You know the street of the theatre of Constantine? Two hours after sunset take this letter and packet to the corner house on the right hand opposite the fountain. At that hour the street is all but deserted, but you will avoid loitering on the way, or speaking to any one you may meet. The packet and letter you must deliver yourself into the hand of the person to whom they are addressed. If you are not admitted, bring them back to me at once; if you are, take especial note of all that passes, of all that you see and hear.

However late the hour, I shall await your report to-night. Do you perfectly understand your instructions?"

"Perfectly," replied the Thracian, with quiet decision.

"Repeat them."

Belisarius did so.

"Until this evening, then," said Justinian; "be silent and cautious; there may be eyes upon you when you least expect it;" and with this significant hint of secrecy dismissed him calmly.

But if Belisarius could have looked back into the room he had just quitted, he would perhaps have been astounded by the sight of his proud, reserved patron lying prone upon the couch, his head buried in his hands and his whole frame shaken by emotion, as he pleaded vehemently with Heaven for the success of his mission to a wanton dancer.

Even so. At last it had come to this. For when Belisarius examined the superscription of the letter, which he did as soon as he was alone in the ante-room, he was taken aback, in spite of his brave resolution to do his duty simply without comment or criticism, to find it was addressed to no other than Theodora, at the house of Chrysomalla the ballet-mistress. We shall learn the contents of that letter somewhat later, and until then let us imitate the gallant Thracian and go on our way, indulging as little as possible in vain surmise or judgment.

One or two points, indeed, presented themselves forcibly to the young man's mind: firstly, that whatever might be his patron's reasons for communicating with Theodora, he had intimated pretty clearly that the affair was to be kept a profound secret—managed, so to speak, upon the sly ; and secondly, that no one could feel himself much more out of his proper vocation than did he, Belisarius, sneaking about the city on nocturnal errands of such a delicate nature, like the sexless dependent of a fine gentleman. There was at least one comfort—this kind of thing would soon be over, and then, hurrah ! for the stride of the war-horse, the rattle of the steel, and the chance of proving himself the man he felt himself to be.

And so with a sigh he accepted his present uncongenial duty and passed out of the anteroom, placing the letter and packet in his bosom. As he did so he received a striking proof of the value of Justinian's caution, for at the very instant a curtain which hung before a lateral doorway was pulled back, and the Lady Lupicina, gaunter and more grim-visaged than ever, made her appearance, followed by a single girl-attendant. Belisarius, somewhat startled at the apparition, saluted the formidable dame and stood still to let her pass; but she also stopped, and scrutinized him sternly from

head to foot. Then in a harsh voice she desired
to know his business there, to which he replied
modestly, that he was on the service of the noble
Justinian. "Ah! I dare say—exactly," said the
Lady Lupicina, nodding her head slowly, and
dropping a syllable out of her severe lips at each
nod. "And who may you be?" The Thracian
gave his name, and the handmaiden ventured to
whisper that it was the brave young man who had
saved the girl from drowning; whereat her mistress
once more looked Belisarius deliberately all over,
remarked to herself aloud, "Hard, hard!" and
shaking her head in as stately a fashion as she had
nodded it, sailed off into her apartments, followed
by the girl, who managed to send over her shoulder
a smile of encouragement to the Thracian, who
probably looked as he felt, rather discomfited by
the old lady's very enigmatical speech and conduct.
Leaving him to meditate upon it as he resumes his
lounge in the court-yard, we shall venture to follow
her.

Arrived in her own chamber the Lady Lupicina
dismissed the girl, with the order that Barsumas was
to attend her instantly; and in due time that worthy,
of whom we have nearly lost sight, made his entry.
The same ruthless fate which had depraved the
rich bass voice of Isidore into an unmelodious roar
had turned the clear falsetto of Barsumas into a
shrill squeak; but while the former champion

found himself forced by circumstances into the
mean position of playing spy for the Cappadocian,
his rival and antagonist had obtained a snug berth
among the domestics of the Lady Lupicina, and
was enabled thereby to strut and swell, and preach
and lord it over his fellow-unfortunates to his
heart's content. Since we last had the misfortune
of being in his company he had grown considerably
less stout, but flabbier and yellower, and more
repulsive-looking than ever. But his notorious
orthodoxy and his sufferings in the cause endeared
him to the Lady Lupicina, and he possessed that
unscrupulous zeal bordering on fanaticism which
in the sixth century—and in many a century since
—was no inconvenient quality in at least one
member of even the best regulated and most
decorous household. ·

His mistress addressed him eagerly directly he
entered. "What have you to report? Have your
agents learnt anything important?"

Barsumas cleared his throat and began. "Noble
lady, the youth Dulcissimus, who was successful in
his watch upon the jeweller, has discovered—through
a handmaiden with whom he is on terms of confidence—that the shameless woman has in all probability accepted the offer of the young Tyrian—
who is given over to destruction—and is likely in
a few days to quit Chrysomalla's house for the one
which he places at her disposal."

"A few days," repeated Lupicina, thoughtfully; " a few days! If only that letter could be intercepted my son might still be saved from the shame he contemplates. His pride would save him then. But how to contrive it? My God! how?"

She concluded with a groan. Barsumas looked at her inquiringly, with a twinkle in his pig eyes.

"Your surmise about the jeweller was right," she continued. "My son was writing and tearing up and writing again all last night. This morning he is pale and haggard; and at this very moment I believe a packet and letter for that accursed woman to be in the hands of the tall young Thracian who has lately entered the household. I saw him from behind the curtain place them in his bosom, and his face—it is an honest one— betrayed his surprise and uneasiness. How to prevent their delivery?"

"The young Thracian?" said Barsumas, gravely. "That is unfortunate. The youth is arrogant and unmannerly, but brave and strong as a lion, and incorruptibly faithful. It is a hard matter."

"Can you suggest nothing?" said Lupicina, angrily; "you, who pretend to be equal to every emergency? Speak, slave, speak! every moment is precious."

"Your Graciousness still declines to sound the Lord Justinian on the subject?"

"I cannot bring myself to do so. I dare not.

I cannot put a barrier of shame between us for
ever. I know him so well—his proud and sensitive
nature. He is more horror-stricken, be sure, at
his own weakness than we can be for him. I have
watched the struggle going on, but I have never
betrayed my knowledge of it. I have kept the secret
even from his mother, from whom I never before
concealed aught that concerned him. But, by God's
mercy, he will get the better of it. If only he were
not so determined when once he has made up his
mind to anything! How often I have gloried in his
firmness, and now it may be his destruction! No,
no, it cannot be! Heaven will not permit a life of
noble purpose to end in miserable failure. The
holy saints are not so heedless of that which is
daily, hourly committed to their charge."

"There is the less reason to doubt that their
blessings will attend your Piety's remonstrances,"
said Barsumas. "The letter may be recalled."

It was a pitiless argument. For a time both
were silent, whilst a desperate conflict went on between the two strong tenants of Lupicina's heart—
her tender, reverential affection for her nephew, and
her implicit trust in celestial guidance and protection. It ended in a manner wholly indefensible, as
such contests sometimes do, a fact which miserable
sinners are more apt to rejoice at than lament over
as they ought. The woman prevailed over the
devotee. Lupicina spoke in a low voice, her hard

grey eye softened by a strangely abstracted look, more as if she were justifying herself to some unseen presence than replying to Barsumas.

"Not for many years," she said, "not since he was a boy at my knee, have I had occasion to disapprove aught in the conduct of my son either in word or deed. I believe that until now there has been no act of his life that he could not have bared to me without a blush. I have not courage to be the first to accuse him of this monstrous thing which he has striven to conceal from human eye, either to his own face or to others. If it be my duty to do so, I humbly pray for pardon in neglecting it, or that he may be spared and a double punishment may fall on me. None—God pardon me for saying it—could be more terrible than to destroy by my own act the pure confidence and sympathy which has ever existed between my son and me. Rather, if the whole city buzzed with the story of his shame, let me be deaf and dumb."

"There remains the alternative," said Barsumas coldly, "of letting matters take their course, and trusting to the arch-harlot's good feeling and the possibility of stifling the scandal."

"And we are to be at her mercy?" gasped Lupicina. "The breath of a shameless dancer, whom the law will not even permit to contaminate with her presence the public baths—who dare not show her face in the theatre except upon the stage she

pollutes—has power to blast the edifice of piety,
learning, and self-control which it has required so
many patient years to perfect! Is this possible?"

"Even so," said Barsumas, quietly. "Of an evil
odour in the fish-market, or a current of blood near
the shambles, men take but small account; but the
suspicion of the one or a spot of the other in the
court of St. Sophia will set men wondering and
gaping."

"And if we look the matter in the face and brave
it out?" said Lupicina, proudly. "Her assertion
against our denial; how many in the city will
choose the former against the latter?"

"If there be but one to begin with, madam,"
replied Barsumas, "in a week there will be ten
thousand. Scandal, gracious lady, is like Greek
fire—inextinguishable; once kindled, it must con-
sume itself and that on which it fastens. Moreover,
your Tenderness is ignoring further action on the
part of the noble Justinian. Lastly, there is the
proof—the letter."

"It is hard to remember that which is so incredible. Can I have been mistaken?"

"I dare not hope so, madam. Depend upon it,
the letter has been written. Granted that it may
be ineffectual, that the fiend will not relinquish her
new victim, the Tyrian; let that letter, whatever
it may contain, be but exhibited—shall we say to
a select circle of scoffers at a supper party——"

"Hush, hush!" cried the unhappy old lady, in an agony of humiliation. No more! For God's sake, no more! What do you propose?"

"It is a hard matter," replied Barsumas, slowly. "Still—still—were that letter not to be delivered until after dusk, as under the circumstances is more than probable, those can be found who will guarantee that the messenger shall never reach his destination."

"'Let us lay wait for blood, let us lurk privily for the innocent,'" quoted Lupicina, sternly. "It is this which you dare ask of me? I will have no bloodshed."

"Your slave would be the last to counsel it. But in such a case as this, where so much is at stake, the most decided measures are excusable."

"No bloodshed," repeated the lady, "nor violence —unnecessary violence."

"No unnecessary violence shall be used," said Barsumas, catching at the permission of the adjective. "But I must remind your Clemency that the Thracian is not one to be cajoled or bribed into betraying his trust, and that to wrest from him that for which he holds himself responsible will require somewhat more force than is needed to take a toy from a fractious child, or a flower from a maiden's bosom."

"It is a terrible alternative," groaned Lupicina, pacing the room in great agitation. "He is a magnificent youth, with honesty and purity in every line of his countenance. Is there no other way?"

"The time is short," said Barsumas, doggedly. "Whilst we are planning, the evil may be accomplished, and my Lord Justinian committed to a folly with which before long all Constantinople will be ringing."

"What has he written?" exclaimed Lupicina. "What can he have proposed? Nothing vile or dishonourable, be certain. He is more noble-minded than we are, than any one."

"Remember the packet, madam," said Barsumas, with a venomous sneer. "Whatever it be, that priestess of hell will not hesitate to proclaim that by her accursed arts she has ensnared the greatest soul amongst us."

"Will you swear that the Thracian's life shall be in no danger?" asked Lupicina, hoarsely. "Can you answer for the ruffians you employ? Speak out; let me know all, without reservation."

"If the matter be placed in my hands," said Barsumas, with almost cheerful alacrity, "I will pledge my own life that he shall receive no permanent injury; but for a time at least it will be forced upon us to incapacitate him from—from further interference. Your Condescension encourages me to speak plainly. I will do so. There is a certain man of the Blue Faction—a desperate character, it must be confessed, but a very artist in his line—who with his own weapon and a fair opportunity will engage to calculate to a fraction the weight of the blow he deals, and in that fraction shall lie the difference between life and death."

"Horrible, horrible!" exclaimed Lupicina, covering her face with her hands. "To what iniquity am I lending myself? That gallant youth!"

"My beloved mistress! consider: reflect, I beseech you, on the shame and ruin which must follow. How will you endure to see your spotless idol bespattered with the filth which every shameless hand will not hesitate to cast upon it—how to hear the howl of derision with which the ungodly greet the perdition of a noble nature—how to meet the despairing sorrow of the righteous, whose faith in their coming champion will be for ever lost? I am no man of blood; I will answer for the Thracian's life. But even were it otherwise—could we purchase secrecy only by the sacrifice of fifty such as he, the bargain would be a cheap one."

"Enough!" groaned Lupicina; "I consent. Act as you think fit. But spare the Thracian, he is but obeying orders."

"Your Graciousness may be easy on that point," said Barsumas, with a furtive gleam on his sallow face. "I will answer for his life and limb. It will be a wholesome lesson for the youth to learn that he is vulnerable, and may teach him discretion. His confidence in himself is somewhat overweening."

"As it ought to be," answered Lupicina, recovering her imperiousness. "It was the same dauntless self-reliance which made my noble husband what he is, which raised his family to its present position. Had you yourself not shown ready courage at a great crisis, you would not now enjoy the confidence of your mistress. Go, and prove yourself worthy of it. Rescue my son from this fatal fancy which has seized him, and deal as gently as may be with that splendid boy. He shall not lack compensation when all is over."

"Ay, ay," said Barsumas, with an affectation of frankness which agreed but ill with his crafty, unwholesome face and thin voice; "a broken head is best mended by a golden plaister. There is many a fine fellow in the city who would gladly agree to the one for the sake of the other at least once a month."

"I can believe it," said Lupicina; "but the Thracian is cast in a different mould to your Faction bravoes. He will think far more of the wound to his honour than the injury to his person. But you swear that the latter shall not be severe?"

"I do, noble lady," said Barsumas. "If all go smoothly, a matter of a day or two at the most."

"And if all do not go smoothly?" asked Lupicina.

Barsumas hesitated.

"I must know the details," said Lupicina, excitedly. "I have consented to the atrocity; speak, and conceal nothing."

"I have suggested, madam, that the letter will not be delivered in all probability before dusk; it would be awkward for our scheme if it were otherwise."

"The messenger may be on his way at this moment!" exclaimed Lupicina, alarmed.

"Believe me, he has not left the court-yard," said Barsumas. "We should have heard of it. Before answering your summons I took the liberty of posting a watch upon his movements, with directions that if anything occurred I was to be communicated with, even in this presence. There is a beggar asking alms not far from the gate, halt and blind, who on occasion might be found to have the full use of his eyes and limbs."

"And these vile agents whom you employ," said Lupicina, "can you depend on their secrecy and good faith?"

"Thanks to the liberal supplies which your Condescension has placed at my disposal, I can; thanks also to a wholesome dread of the Prefect of the city. Their lives for the most part contain episodes concerning which his Eminence would be glad of information."

"We shall be able to say much the same of our own," said Lupicina, bitterly.

Barsumas bowed and continued. " The Thracian will scarcely anticipate danger on his errand. He will be as unprepared for attack as it is in his nature to be. The street is dark and full of convenient recesses. In passing one of these he receives a single blow from Pausanias, is stunned for the moment—nothing more. Possibly he falls. When he recovers himself the letter and packet are missing. Before long we shall learn their contents, and at least gain time to decide upon future plans."

" Base and cowardly ! " moaned Lupicina.

" But the only way," replied Barsumas, " unless your Graciousness will undertake remonstrance."

" Anything rather than that," said Lupicina, firmly. " And the name you mentioned ? "

" The Pausanias, madam ? " said Barsumas, blandly ; " the care-calmer ? That is the weapon."

" What is it like ? "

" My noble mistress, why distress yourself with these details ? "

" What is it like ? " repeated Lupicina, savagely.

" The Pausanias, madam, is a muffled cudgel of peculiar shape and flexibility. It does its work silently, and is rarely fatal unless wielded by an inexperienced hand. There is no time to lose. I have your permission to make the necessary arrangements ? "

In a scarcely audible tone Lupicina replied, " So be it," and pointed to the door.

The eunuch, bowing, left the room. As he passed a window over the court-yard he peeped stealthily out, and saw the tall form of Belisarius leaning against one of the pillars, a model of athletic grace.

"Insolent young upstart!" growled Barsumas; "we will take some of the assurance out of him before the night is over."

In presenting this painful spectacle of an elderly lady renowned for piety and integrity betraying her weakness, and, rather than undergo the torture of condemning her idol, consenting to become an accomplice in a base and inexcusable action, with the hope that good might come of it, I must once more remind my horrified readers that after all Lupicina was but a Dacian peasant, the sister of a man who, although a general of the empire, could neither read nor write, and that all these things happened in the far-off sixth century. Moreover, as the law of retribution is fixed and immutable, in due time Lupicina reaped the whirlwind. Meanwhile we leave her, too, upon her knees before her favourite saint, confessing her culpable weakness and praying fervently that no very serious consequences might result from it, and that in the end all might turn out for the best.

CHAPTER III.

IN THE NICK OF TIME.

AT the moment when Lupicina was deciding that
to permit the outrage upon Belisarius was prefer-
able to wounding her own feelings and those of her
nephew, John of Cappadocia was again closeted
with Chrysomalla. That very morning Isidore had
accidentally discovered for his employer a fact with
which we are already acquainted, namely, that the
mysterious individual against whom he was constantly running in his capacity as spy, was an
agent in the service of Barsumas. As he knew the
position of the latter in Lupicina's household, the
quick wits of the Cappadocian soon followed up
the clue. He divined that the old lady had, like
himself, penetrated Justinian's secret. Here was
a fresh complication. The question arose whether
it would pay better to depart from the original
programme and to assist the dragon in the
protection of her treasure.

Having a claim on the confidence of Alexander the jeweller, which the latter found it well worth his while to recognize, John learnt that Justinian had ordered the bracelet to be sent back to him, with the sapphire set in the place of the lost emerald. He was therefore clearly meditating some serious step. It could only be with the manifest intention of establishing relations with Theodora. With what aim and to what extent? It was at least comprehensible that, being such as he was, he should go to work in an underhand, shamefaced manner, which an ordinary man of the world would laugh to scorn; but it was impossible that he, the observed of all men, could expect to make the acquaintance of a notorious public character like the dancer, and to keep the fact hidden from society for more than twenty-four hours. In spite of his mature age he might be a novice in such matters, but he was the reverse of a fool, and none but a hopeless fool could anticipate such miraculous immunity from scandal.

At first sight, then, it appeared that Justinian was on the point of degrading himself to the level of a mere libertine, and of sacrificing the immaculate reputation of years to the indulgence of a gross caprice; and this not in one of those moments of fiery temptation to which the most saintlike of men have at times succumbed, but with cool and mature resolve. John's mind had scarcely admitted this supposition before he rejected it unreservedly as absurd, and set himself with his usual determination to evolve the solution of the problem.

And now his inclination to believe that above the white brow and chestnut tresses of fair, shameless Theodora hovered the hitherto invisible diadem of honour and prosperity, which the stars had promised to the house of Acacius, returned with double force. His powerful intellect forcing itself for the moment above the leaden atmosphere of cunning and intrigue which habitually paralyzed its nobler efforts, soared with all the audacity of inspired vision. He surveyed the future with marvellous breadth and boldness of conception, grasped at its huge, salient possibilities, and accepted them as probable, contemptuously ignoring the antagonistic minutiæ of circumstance. In these rare moods John's nature attained grandeur. It developed the sublime of credulity; the capacity for infinite belief in the conceivable ; a large measure of that faculty which in every crisis of the world's progress has enabled individuals to serenely contemplate and undauntedly affirm the likelihood of some contingency which the universal voice proclaimed monstrously improbable, if not impossible ; in defiance of tradition, prejudice, experience, and the respectable quality called common sense—too often a synonym for stupidity and narrowness of mind;

despite of being branded for the time as credulous, as impostors, as fanatic dreamers; of being invariably laughed to scorn, often persecuted, sometimes martyred. Credulity has been contemptuously defined as a disposition to believe on insufficient evidence, as if in that very insufficiency did not lie the glory of the belief. It is the "faith" of the apostle, "the substance of things hoped for, the evidence of things not seen." That which in the one or the few is credulity becomes faith in the many, but the former has all the grandeur of originality, the latter the insignificance of plagiarism. Credulity established Christianity, helped to discover America, and supported George Stephenson against all England. Faith enables us to gabble complacently through the dogmas of the Creed in chorus every Sunday; to await calmly the discovery of the North Pole, and the completion of a railway to India: but the one is a sequel to the other; the one results from education and experience, the other from irrepressible inward conviction.

There is no desire to claim for John of Cappadocia a resemblance to the above-mentioned heroic enthusiasts, further than at certain moments he manifested a similar range and hardihood of conception. Had he in his hour of inspiration chanced to arrive at any conclusion likely to be of practical utility, he was too selfish, too entirely devoted to

the one idea of self-aggrandisement, to promulgate
it for the benefit of mankind, unless by so doing
he could secure the lion's share of the profits;
far too wary and politic to endanger his reputation
for foresight by submitting a crude idea to public
criticism.

As it was, he had merely eliminated out of the
depths of his semi-heathenish, semi-atheistic philosophy the perception of certain fanciful ideas,
which at the same time were truths, and truths
which even a tolerant and liberal-minded Christian
—supposing such a being to have existed in Constantinople—might have accepted without shame:
that the merciless condemnation of society did not
necessitate the total perdition of the criminal; that
in the most polluted and degraded soul there may
lurk some redeeming grace, some ineradicable germ
of nobility which is equivalent to a galaxy of
orthodox and stereotyped virtues, and which may
eventually expand into grandeur; and that if there
is one thing more prone to downfall than another,
it is an elaborate system of piety and learning
which persistently tramples on nature and despises
the shortcomings of others.

But these notions John worked out by sheer force
of his uncompromising fatalism, unhampered by
any recognition of conventional ethics, of right and
wrong, punishment and reward, and the like. He
saw the truth and the light, but he saw it as—if we

believe the tradition—in the court of British Arthur, about the same date, the grosser spirits of the Round Table saw the Holy Grail, a phantom of itself, pale and shrouded from their unworthy vision.

But he saw, notwithstanding. He saw Theodora, in defiance of the world's pitiless sentence, to the confusion of all theory and calculation, and the discomfiture of the wise and prudent, toiling desperately through by-ways of ineffable iniquity, and hideous gulfs of shame illumined by the glare of infernal fires, to emerge at last triumphant and fulfil the decree of destiny. He saw Justinian laboriously striving to exalt himself into the perfect man; patiently fortifying himself by years of study and self-denial, and crying, in the pride of his heart, "My citadel is impregnable," and under the same irresistible impulse of fate creeping forth from his stronghold in fear and trembling—but not without a strange, unaccountable hope—to seek his counterpart in the very mire!

And then, with the vulture instinct strong within him, he debated how best all this might serve the turn of John of Cappadocia, and dropping from his height in the clouds hurried off to a consultation with Chrysomalla.

He found his innocent-faced, vicious-hearted confederate in a state of despondent resignation at the prospect of losing her lodger. "At the same time," she said plaintively, "I always knew it must come to this, and bold as I am she frightens me sometimes."

" What may have been her last success in that line ? " asked John, smiling.

" She gave me a very strong hint that she suspected there was some trickery about that closet—you know, where I placed you to listen, the day Ecebolus was here."

" How did she do it ? "

" Well, I told you that she has every sort of present sent to her, and takes a fancy to all kinds of things that no woman ever took a fancy to before. The other day I went into her room and found her examining—what do you suppose? A bow! I don't know who gave it to her, but it seems it was of some rare wood, or perhaps horn, mounted in gold, and came from Persia. 'Look here, Chrysomalla,' she said ; ' do you think I could bend this ? ' ' Never, my dear,' said I ; ' and don't try, or you'll strain yourself. Our young ladies all carried bows when we did Diana and Actæon, but they were mere toys. That's a man's bow, and a strong man's too ! ' 'I think I could, though,' she answered, and fitted an arrow with a great barbed head on the string. ' What shall I shoot at ? ' On the panel of that closet inside her room there is a painted figure of Pan dancing and playing on a pipe. ' Look out, Pan ! ' she cried, and in a moment straightened her long white arm, bent the bow like a reed, and whiz went the arrow right through the middle of Pan, and disappeared. 'How thin the wall is!' said she, laughing; 'it would have been disagreeable for any one on the other side. Now I've spoilt the panel don't trouble to get it mended; it will do to practise at.' And then she laid the bow down. Only fancy if you had been there!"

"It would have served me right," said John, candidly. "How admirable she is! Certainly the hint was unmistakable. And now about Ecebolus. Is everything settled between those two?"

"I believe so," said Chrysomalla, "but I am not certain. I don't like to be too inquisitive, and of course she may change her mind. I should not be surprised at anything she did. If she were to walk in at this very minute and announce that she was going to turn abbess, or marry the Patriarch, I should scarcely be astonished."

"Can you tell me one thing?" said John. "Has that bracelet ever put in an appearance again?"

"Now, I do wonder what you are about," returned Chrysomalla. "You are so profound! I have always considered myself as deep as most people, but I am as shallow to you as the little Lycus is to the Bosphorus. No, I have heard nothing of it. By the way, what on earth am I

to say if it does turn up and I have to answer
questions?"

"Tell the exact truth for once," said John;
"say that I carried it off. You have nothing to
do with its return."

"That is cool," said Chrysomalla, "considering
it is my property. How about the fifty gold
pieces I lose by it?"

"How about that emerald?" retorted John,
blandly. "Come, don't let us two squabble. Be
patient, and you shall have no reason to complain."

"Of course I was only joking, sir," said Chrysomalla, coquettishly. "You know I admire you
and trust you, which possibly few people do; and
therefore you find it difficult to believe. But so it
is. I acknowledge you as my master; you are so
delightfully and calmly wicked. Is there anything
else in which I can oblige you? You won't let me
into your secret, I suppose?"

"Not just yet."

Chrysomalla pouted.

"My plans may come to nothing," continued
the Cappadocian, "and I am afraid of being
laughed at."

"Ah! I daresay," said Chrysomalla; "poor
timid thing! As if we don't all have our failures
as well as our successes. My Leda, now, was a
triumph; but as Diana I fell flat. I never looked
as if I could have run after anything, even a

tortoise. That short tunic is very trying to some people."

John's hawk eyes were glistening with merriment as he pictured the round pink-and-white creature before him aspiring to represent the long-limbed Artemis.

"Let us for ever abjure short tunics," he said, solemnly. "My case is similar. I am attempting to play Mercury; my figure is against me, and I dread falling flat!"

"Mercury! Mercury! Let me see. We brought him into something once; he was—— "

"Patron of cleverness and cunning; of the inventive and acquisitive tendencies; encourager of trade, and general go-between."

Chrysomalla shook her pert head doubtfully. "You are too much for me," she said. "I know you are quizzing me somehow; but it is no use being angry with a man like you. Have you anything serious to say?"

"I have. To entreat you that if you should happen to hear anything about the bracelet, you will at once send off that young rascal Philotarion with a letter for me—sealed, remember—whatever the hour may be—by night or by day. He will hear of me either at home or at the office."

"God bless me! you are serious!" exclaimed Chrysomalla. "Oh! I would give a great deal to know what you are up to."

"My dear Chrysomalla," said John, "is it needful for me to press upon *you* the importance of being discreet? And——"

"There, there! you may stop. I'm not a fool. Trust me for not spoiling sport: but being a woman I must and will be curious."

"You shall be," said John, soothingly; "and in any reasonable way I am willing to gratify you."

With a great deal that followed this amicable adjustment of feminine prerogative we have no concern, as it does not bear upon our story. It was some time after nightfall when John rose and said, "I must be off; my tame rogue will be waiting for me outside. I ordered him to meet me." And so left the house.

As he stepped into the narrow street, lying half in shadow, half in moonlight, he gave a low whistle, and presently out of some dark corner close by appeared Isidore, and joined his patron. The two stood muttering together until their attention was attracted by the sound of a footfall coming down the street. "Step back into the shadow," said the Cappadocian, "and keep still. We will let him pass."

It was a man who with a firm stride came swinging along in the moonlight on the opposite side of the way. Before long he was near enough for them to make out his tall figure sliding past the white walls. Presently he was swallowed up

for a moment by a little gulf of blackness caused
by a retiring portico; and as he emerged from it
the watchers heard a faint thud, saw him reel into
the street and fall, while two dark shadows sprang
out of the gloom behind, and could be seen
stooping over him as he lay.

John of Cappadocia was a man of high courage,
and in his ponderous frame lay great physical
strength. He knew that he could depend on
Isidore, with whose prowess we are already acquainted, and that the latter never stirred abroad
at night without the stout cudgel which had served
him so well on sundry other occasions. To do
the Cappadocian justice, he would scarcely have
hesitated an instant in going to the rescue of
anybody under the circumstances; but, in addition
to this natural impulse, something in the gait and
bearing of the figure had seemed familiar to him
even in the uncertain light, and there flashed
across him a vague suspicion of the truth. Therefore, bidding Isidore follow him, he sprang forward
at once. The ex-chorister, whose lungs were still
capable of uttering a fearful and stentorian roar,
raised the war-cry of his Faction, "Green to the
rescue," and brandishing his cudgel dashed after
his patron, who, had time permitted, would most
certainly have objected to this superfluous uproar.

Meanwhile the victim of the outrage seemed to
have still left in him a certain power of dead

resistance, for one of the ruffians exclaimed, "Curse the obstinate devil! I can't loosen his clutch. If I hadn't sworn like an idiot not to use my knife! Give him another touch of Pausanias!"

"He's got as much as I dare give him," answered his comrade. "I've done my part well enough, and if you were not such a bungling fool you'd have done yours. By hell! here's a rescue. Here come the Greens! Look alive, damn you! Remember our orders; if they take us we are lost men!"

Possibly the terrific war-cry of Isidore, reverberated by the buildings, might have suggested the presence of a whole army of Greens; possibly the ruffians' orders were imperative—not to show fight or risk detection. Anyhow, before John and his follower came up, the more cautious bravo was in rapid retreat, and his fellow, making one more violent and abortive attempt to secure that for which he was searching, struck the fallen man a tremendous blow on the temple with his clenched fist, and with a savage oath took to his heels also.

In the tall form lying senseless before him, John at once recognized the youth who had rescued Antonina from drowning, and had since entered Justinian's service. The last cowardly blow had completed the work of the bludgeon, and if administered sooner might have saved the striker some trouble. Belisarius lay quite motionless ; his face, turned to the moonlight, was set in a resolute frown, and his broad, sinewy hands were still clenched over his chest.

"Have they killed him?" asked Isidore, as the Cappadocian gently detached from their hold the now passive fingers.

"His heart still beats," said John; "he is only stunned. Go at once to Chrysomalla's and procure assistance. We must carry him in there before the neighbours are roused. Quick!"

Directly he was left alone John took out of the bosom of the Thracian's tunic the letter and packet, glanced at the direction of the former, and deliberately transferred them to his own garments.

CHAPTER IV.

A FRIEND IN NEED.

The whole night Justinian waited for Belisarius—
sleepless, and a prey to a hundred anxious thoughts.
It was broad daylight before it was announced to
him that the young man had returned, having
been attacked and seriously maltreated, but that,
although still weak and suffering, he requested an
immediate audience.

In a few minutes Justinian heard from the
Thracian's own lips the particulars of the outrage:
that he received a tremendous blow from behind
and fell all but paralyzed, yet with sufficient consciousness to feel some one trying to tear open the
breast of his tunic, and that he concentrated his
remaining strength in grasping the packet and
letter with both hands; that he fancied he heard
shouts and steps approaching, but received a second
blow which rendered him completely senseless;
that, on recovering, he found himself lying in

Chrysomalla's house, attended by that lady herself and her domestics, when he discovered the packet and the letter to be missing, and was informed that the attack had been witnessed by certain passengers in the street who ran to his succour, when his assailants made off; that his rescuers had carried him into the nearest house, and, finding he was likely to be well cared for, took their departure as soon as he showed signs of coming to himself.

About the same time Barsumas, with as long a face as it was possible to assume, was breaking to Lupicina the miscarriage of their plot.

It is hard to describe the feelings of either aunt or nephew: Lupicina, horrified to find that the crime she had sanctioned had actually in a manner brought about the end it was intended to prevent, for one of the bravoes reported that, on sneaking back to watch the issue of affairs, he had seen Belisarius carried into Chrysomalla's house;—Justinian, tortured by the conviction that the outrage upon his messenger had been deliberately planned, that the packet and letter had fallen into hostile hands, and might be used against him at any moment and for any purpose, political or otherwise.

In the mean time John of Cappadocia remained master of the situation. After luxuriating in the consciousness of this fact for a single day, he decided upon playing the bold game, and commencing operations at once upon Justinian in person.

On the rare occasions when the two had met since their conversation under the chestnut trees, the subject of Theodora and her bracelet had never been revived; indeed, it had been part of John's policy to avoid any interview at which such confidential topics might be possible. But in the mind of Justinian the image of the Cappadocian was inseparably associated with each event as it had occurred, and now in the agony of his suspense he felt instinctively that some understanding was necessary and inevitable between himself and that massive, inscrutable man with the hawk eyes and heavy jaw.

With this idea uppermost in his mind, he was all the more startled at receiving John's request for an interview on matters of importance. At the same time, a sudden hope and sense of relief which he experienced made him aware how strong had been his desire for such an opportunity. It is only the stateliest type of intellect which is entirely self-sufficient, and capable under every fortune of standing aloof from sympathy and companionship. This isolated equanimity was really beyond Justinian, although to attain it had been the great ambition of his life. Possibly he realized at last that by him it was unattainable, for throughout his grand career nothing was more remarkable than his wise selection of subordinates and instruments. As we have learnt, his power of reading human nature was very great; he contrived to attach to himself a group of men wholly distinct in temperament and character, and not always distinguished by a lofty standard of ethics, yet each and all possessing some marked quality not seldom corresponding to a deficiency in himself, and thus solidified his personality, as a main building is strengthened with buttresses.

At this period of his life he was too sensitive and reserved to seek openly for counsel and assistance. Nevertheless, at the sound of the Cappadocian's heavy step, he felt not unlike a man who, struggling in vain to extricate himself from a pitfall, hears of a sudden a voice bidding him be of good heart, and sees a strong hand held down to his succour.

Something of this satisfaction must have been reflected in his face and the tone of his courteous welcome, for John, who in spite of his native effrontery had been troubled with doubts as to his reception, became at once reassured, and without much preamble plunged confidently into the matter on hand.

"Two nights back, sir," he said, "a member of your household was attacked in the street, and I fear seriously maltreated."

"His injuries were only superficial," said Justinian, "and I am glad to say he is now doing well."

"I happened to be passing that way," continued John, "and was lucky enough to arrive in time to rescue him from his assailants, but not before he was insensible."

"It is to you, then, that our thanks for such timely assistance are due," said Justinian, with much cordiality. "I have no doubt, from his account, that in another minute the miscreants would have murdered him outright."

"Possibly on account of his gallant conduct; but I am inclined to believe that their original intention did not go beyond robbery. Directly I arrived at the spot I recognized him as the young man who saved the girl Antonina from drowning, opposite the Villa Ecebolus, when the boat was upset by Porphyrio, and I knew that, owing to his behaviour on that occasion, he had been honoured by the position of confidential domestic in your household."

"An honour," said Justinian, "which he scarcely appreciates, for in a few days he leaves my service to join a cavalry regiment. I can hardly blame him, however, for if ever a youth were intended by nature for a soldier, he is."

"A man can only fulfil his destiny," said John, sententiously, "and must obey its impulses. If he live to be a man in years, as he is already in strength and courage, we may expect that he will make a name for himself one of these days."

"He has heroic qualities," assented Justinian. "But forgive me; I am interrupting your account. You say that when you arrived he was insensible."

"Exactly; and even in that state his hands were tightly clenched over something concealed in his bosom, which I, therefore, at once concluded to be of value and importance, and to have furnished the reason for the attack upon him."

Justinian bent his head without venturing upon speech.

John proceeded. "I sent my servant to procure assistance from the nearest house, which happened to be that of Chrysomalla, and then, seeing that your domestic was no longer capable of protecting that which had been given into his charge, upon the impulse of the moment I took the liberty of transferring it to my own, dreading lest it might fall into curious and unscrupulous hands, and be used for improper ends. I beg of you, Noble sir, to forgive me if I erred in judgment or am mistaken in my conjectures, and, in any case, to rely on my perfect discretion."

And with these words John quietly produced the letter and the packet, and laid them upon the table.

The immediate offer of the Imperial diadem would not have been half so grateful to Justinian as was the sight of those two neat parcels with the seals unbroken and the strings intact. No one ignorant of his great self-command, and noting his easy tone and manner, and the natural interest, perfectly devoid of eagerness, with which he had listened to the Cappadocian, could possibly have guessed the tortures of apprehension and doubt he had undergone during the last two days. But now these were at an end, or rather they were condensed into the endurable fact that a single man had by some means discovered his secret, and had been bold enough to come and tell him so to his very face—possibly not without some ulterior regard to his own profit, but still in a manner unmistakably friendly and delicate; and the one man, moreover, in whom, if some confidence was necessary, he would have elected to confide. He had been irresistibly attracted by John's large-viewed, tolerant sagacity, and was not alarmed by his subtlety. No enemy would have voluntarily resigned a weapon which he might have used with deadly effect. If he were a friend, the more subtle the better; if neutral, at the worst he was looking for his price.

With these reflections passing rapidly through his mind he spoke.

"I thank you from the bottom of my heart. You have acted with excellent judgment, and, I confess, relieved me from a great anxiety."

"In my turn, sir," said John, "I thank you sincerely for those words, which afford me also infinite relief and satisfaction. I did trust that, under the circumstances, my visit might not be unacceptable; at the same time, I could not but reflect that I laid myself open to the charge of being inexcusably officious."

"Pray dismiss any such idea," replied Justinian. "In the restoration of that letter you have done me a great service, since it seems that it would not have passed directly to the person for whom it was intended. Had it fallen, as you suggested, into unscrupulous hands, the consequences might have been serious."

"May I, then, sir, presume so far upon your graciousness as to suggest that in sending a letter at all to such a quarter there was terrible imprudence?"

"Your courtesy makes you a lenient critic," said Justinian. "You might reasonably use a stronger term, and pronounce the writer a madman; and it might be a fairer rendering of your thoughts."

"No," said John, quietly. "My words expressed my full thought. The letter *per se* might be a proof of superior wisdom."

"To be the writer of such a letter at all," said Justinian," presupposes faith in certain qualities in the recipient. Had it been duly delivered I anticipated no danger."

"I understand," said John; "only in case of miscarriage. Such, to a great extent, was my own meaning. I am, sir, perhaps one of the very small minority in this city who would allow your confidence to be not altogether misplaced."

These few exchanges were of great use to the Cappadocian. They confirmed his opinion as to the contents of the letter.

"I will not insult you," said Justinian, "by ascribing your presence here to the operation of pure chance. If I accuse you of premeditated interference in my affairs it is only to compliment your acuteness. I intend to be candid with you, and I shall be happy if I can inspire a reciprocity of candour on your part. A short time ago I should have shrunk from the idea of discussing this subject with any human being. To avoid it would now be absurd on my part. You force me to recognize your knowledge of a secret which I believed to be securely guarded in my own breast. By restoring the proofs of that secret you as forcibly negative the suspicion that your motives are otherwise than friendly, if not—pardon me—altogether disinterested. That would be too much to expect. Disinterestedness is not an attribute of any sensible person in these days."

John smiled approvingly, with a bow of assent to the last proposition.

"I am therefore led to the conclusion that in seeking me personally you have some special object in view beyond the friendly act by which you have laid me under an obligation. I shall be very glad if by speaking thus I can induce you to explain clearly what that object may be."

Justinian had exposed himself to the first thrust. It was, of course, open to the Cappadocian to be offended by his remarks, and to disclaim any but the simplest motives of honesty and civility. John appreciated the intentional unguardedness, and answered frankly.

"A very simple one. You make explanation easy, sir. My hope—forgive my presumption—is to establish between us relations somewhat fuller than those of mere acquaintanceship."

"So I imagined," said Justinian, with some caustic emphasis. "I am bound to feel flattered by the proposal. I will not deny that for a man like myself, apt to indulge overmuch in barren theory, the contact with a strong, practical mind like your own might be wholesome; but as a reciprocity of interest is indispensable to such a connection, I am justified in asking what personal benefit you hope to derive from it."

"My own advancement," said John, bluntly.

Justinian smiled at this candid admission. "You are ambitious," he said. "You have succeeded while still a young man in obtaining—by your own exertions, as far as I know—an honourable and lucrative position. It does not content you?"

"For the moment, yes. It places me in easy circumstances and gives me regular occupation, but it has no stability and no future. It is dependent on the favour of a government which, in its turn, exists only on the precarious tenure of an old man's life."

Justiaian thought it as well to ignore the full purport of this last sentence. " You might reasonably expect," he said, " that any government would recognize your merit and be glad to retain your services."

" Such is, in fact, my hope," said John, calmly ; " and it is for that very reason that I have ventured to address myself to the certain source of all future honour and reward."

This was plain speaking, and a pause followed.

Justinian felt that they were on dangerous ground, and suspected a trap. To entangle a man in his talk, and afterwards accuse him of treasonable designs against the government, was a favourite practice with the political agents in those days even when the accused was of no especial importance, but, nevertheless, better out of the way. Although he had hitherto taken no active share in public matters, and, politically speaking, led a life of absolute seclusion, Justinian knew himself to be a marked man—an object of jealousy and suspicion to the Imperial party and the Green Faction generally, who earnestly desired that Hypatius should succeed his uncle on the throne. A weak prince must needs be blind to the excesses of the

party to whom he owes his elevation, and with
Hypatius as Emperor the Greens promised themselves a perpetuity of Saturnalia. Against their
mighty organization and the obstinate animosity of
Anastasius, even the ægis of Justin and his guards
might be powerless to oppose a charge of treason
seriously pressed and backed by a sufficient amount
of hard swearing.

As a set-off to these suspicions was the fact that
John had given up the letter addressed to Theodora,
which, even if he supposed it to be a mere declaration of passion, he might fairly have hoped to use
with terrible effect in destroying Justinian's prestige
with his own party, and nullifying that character
for sanctified reserve which, together with his reputation for learning, had gained him the respect
even of his enemies. Still, as every one knew, a
man could not be imprisoned or exiled for inditing
an epistle to an actress, and the apparently friendly
action might be a cheap cloak for treachery. Had
John actually known the contents of the letter
would he have then restored it ?

The instinct of the Cappadocian, the ex-informer,
read a part of that which was passing in Justinian's
mind. It entertained him to reflect how often, without exciting suspicion, he had done exactly that of
which he was now suspected, when, for the first time
in his life, probably, he was acting with sincerity.
He was equal to the occasion. While Justinian,

with a searching look in his prominent eyes, was meditating an answer, he spoke again with a frank laugh.

"Ah, forgive my awkwardness. I see I have alarmed you. My declaration was too abrupt. I well understand your hesitation, sir; we live in times when a man cannot be too much on his guard. But I beseech you to believe that my duties as Prætorian secretary do not oblige me to supply the government with secret information." And John laughed again, like a man much tickled with an idea but in no wise offended.

Justinian reddened. It is always humiliating to find one's thoughts anticipated and one's misgivings turned into a jest. But he did not condescend to a denial.

"I have heard it whispered," he said, "that your accomplishments include an acquaintance with the magic art. I shall begin to believe it. Not content with discovering my secrets, you even penetrate my thoughts. It is an enviable gift, but not possessing it, I must in self-defence resort to the poor expedient of asking questions. Are you willing to gratify my curiosity on one or two points?"

"On fifty, if you please," said John, "if by so doing I can overcome your natural distrust of a comparative stranger."

"I will not put your talent to the proof by asking

you to read the contents of a sealed letter, but you
will probably guess what is inside that packet."

" The bracelet, of course."

" The test is too easy," said Justinian.

" In the place of the lost emerald," continued
John quietly, " there is now a sapphire; blue has
displaced green."

" That is marvellous ! " exclaimed Justinian,
startled out of his serene demeanour.

" And, like most marvels, open to simple solution.
I saw the bracelet at the jeweller's."

" Then that double-faced Greek betrayed me ! "

" Do not be too hard on poor Alexander," said
John, laughingly; "he is the soul of discretion, and
would rather become bankrupt than betray the
secrets of his customers. But I was once lucky
enough to save him from the clutches of the law,
and since then he has been my devoted slave."

"You have laid your toils skilfully," said Justinian
with some bitterness; "there is no escape from
them. I scarcely despair of hearing my letter
repeated word for word."

A rare opportunity for a tactician, a fatal one
for a bungler ! The very crisis of the game ! John
felt that on his reply depended in a great measure
his chance of securing Justinian's favour. He had
spent some hours during the previous day in trying
to picture to himself the kind of letter which a
man like Justinian would write to a woman like

Theodora, and during the interview had carefully estimated the value of every syllable which had reference to it. Was Justinian's undisguised satisfaction at its return entirely attributable to the fear lest a paragon of propriety might have been detected in declaring his admiration for a popular dancer, or was there some weighter reason still ?

" The letter ? " said John ; " that is a very different matter. There, indeed, I have no accomplice, and must rely upon my own fallible intelligence. It shrinks from the ordeal, and yet—and yet——"

" And yet ? " repeated Justinian.

John shook his head. " I have not courage to make the attempt."

" To fail could scarcely be considered a disgrace," said Justinian. " I shall find out now," he thought, " if this man can understand me."

John's reply came in a deep, vibrating murmur, as if he were communing with himself.

" Hope for the condemned, pity for the victim, admiration for the artist, horror of the wanton, love for the woman ! "

A shiver passed over Justinian, but he remained silent.

" Yes ! " continued the Cappadocian, in the same rich monotone. " No idle sentimentalism, no commonplace rhapsody, no grossness of diction, no impurity of thought. Nothing that could lower or

shame the writer, much that might elevate the
reader; sentiments too lofty for ignoble compre-
hensions, yet intelligible to the diviner essence
which even degradation and licentiousness cannot
annihilate; no weak sympathy with evil, but an
intense desire to impute good; a tender recognition
of all that is redeeming, generous extenuation of
the past, encouragement for the future—encouragement, possibly, too daring not to be dangerous if
interpreted by malicious eyes."

As John concluded, Justinian gave a great sigh
of relief, or satisfaction, or perhaps both. Then
he took up the small roll of paper, and began
slowly breaking the seals and strings.

"I have always believed myself," he said, "to be
as impenetrable as my neighbours, and decidedly
not liable to be suspected of certain weaknesses to
which most men are prone. I am anxious to know
what first supplied you with a clue."

"The simple exercise of my wits," said John,
rousing himself and resuming his matter-of-fact
tone. "Like many a good man before me, I
arrived in Constantinople with little else besides
them to depend upon; necessity is a good whet-
stone. But I had special reasons—pardon my
audacity—for observing you narrowly. I have
been an adventurer, sir, in the fullest sense of the
word. I confess myself one still, although in saying so I grossly insult the majesty of the depart-

ment in which I have the honour to hold a post, and your courtesy will not wound the feelings of my worthy chief by repeating my words to him."

"Have no fear on that score," said Justinian, laughing.

"I can think of no better way to enlighten you, sir, on this and sundry other points, than by giving you a short sketch of my life since my arrival in the city, if I thought that it would not try your patience intolerably."

"On the contrary; I shall listen with the greatest interest," said Justinian, with perfect truth.

But John's confessions claim another chapter.

CHAPTER V.

AN ADVENTURER.

"You were pleased to observe, sir," said John, "that you had heard me suspected of dabbling in the black art. The suspicion, if it goes too far, has still a certain base of truth. When I was very young, and possibly very foolish, I employed—or must I say wasted?—a good deal of the time which should have been devoted to preparation for the bar in studies which by no pretence could be construed as legal, and especially in mastering the most fascinating—to myself, at least—of all the occult sciences, astrology. Whether I ever believed that it would be of service to me in later life I can scarcely say; but you may understand that at the time I was in earnest, when I tell you that I expended the greater part of my very moderate allowance in buying up all the old treatises and manuscripts upon the subject which I could lay hands on, stinting myself in every possible manner to gratify this one passion."

"That is indeed a convincing proof," said Justinian, smiling.

"You smile, sir. You have never known what it is to be at once an enthusiast and a pauper. But perhaps you altogether despise the science on which I bestowed my early affections and pocket money, or, like many persons, consider the attempts of a wretched mortal to investigate the future as rank impiety."

"I should be sorry," said Justinian, gravely, " to despise any pursuit which has a noble science for its basis; nor is it for me to limit the sources of enlightenment which the Divine wisdom may think fit to reveal to human reason. As to magic there cannot be two opinions; to seek for knowledge by confessedly diabolical agency is to court certain perdition, and for the sinner who attempts it there can be neither mercy here nor hereafter. But it is hard to think that communion with the celestial bodies is in itself an evil thing, although it is liable to terrible abuse. Were it possible to strip the study of astrology of its paganism, or to regard them as of merely technical utility, and to approach it solely in the spirit of philosophic research, fortified by Christian principle, it might cease to be a dangerous pursuit. But there lies the difficulty. The very necessity of constantly pondering on the heathenish jargon which astrology affects must produce an unwholesome habit of thought. Who will dare to affirm that he cannot be seduced into arrogance and infidelity? Who amongst us is proof against temptation?" And Justinian concluded his sermon with a sigh.

"Allowing the risk," said John, "do you think it impossible that there might be results valuable enough to justify one in incurring it?"

"To most men I should give an unqualified answer —nothing can *justify* a man in incurring even a fractional risk to his soul. But with you I will not dogmatize. If it be true that the stars have some mysterious connection with and power over human existence—and many wise and pious men have asserted it—it can only be by Divine permission. Their influence must be a procession of Providence. A pagan may stumble on a truth, and it may be none the less a truth for the false creed of its discoverer; but in the present age we are bound to Christianize its application. Can this be done? Can it be done with safety? If a faint light glimmer through the veil of the future, is it not rather to test our humility and discretion than to tempt our ambition and curiosity? Let us pause lest, bewildered by the unwonted light, we find our feet entangled by the snares which the arch-enemy is ever at such moments spreading before us. That which was undertaken with pure resolve and loftiest motives may be perverted to the basest ends; the enthusiast may degenerate into a schemer, the sage into a charlatan, the prophet to a liar, the searcher after sublime truths into the author of infernal sophistries."

"What a terrible habit he has of moralizing!" was John's inward reflection; "one-third conviction and the rest conceit. It is a useful thing at times, but there is a limit.—After hearing your sentiments, sir," he said aloud, "it would be hardly fair on myself to continue my confessions. I am bound to be accounted either fool or knave."

"By no means," said Justinian, hastily. "I beg of you to continue. Do not misunderstand me. I know that I am a pitiless theorist, and when the fit is on me I must have my say; but if I seem intolerant in my speech, I trust that at heart I am not so. Pray continue, and let your narrative be as outspoken and matter of fact as may be. You will lay me under another obligation. The experiences of an adventurous, energetic life like your own cannot fail to be of service to a dreamer like myself."

"So be it, sir," said John. "You may count upon my speaking plainly; and if, as is most probable, I both horrify and disgust you, my candour must plead in extenuation. To resume, then. I passed through the usual course at Berytus, paid a flying visit to the courts of Athens, and arrived in Constantinople with the small remnant of my patrimony, a respectable store of musty manuscripts, a fair smattering of legal knowledge, and an inexhaustible stock of impudence and self-confidence. I had scarcely settled in the city, in a humble way enough, before I began to carry out my favourite maxim that a man cannot know too much of his neighbours' affairs. Without money or position it is hard to make decent acquaintances, much less friends; but I persevered after my own fashion. By degrees it came to be whispered among the many with whom I came in contact that something beyond a mere dry legal opinion might be obtained from the strange-looking Cappadocian. The majority, perhaps, ridiculed the idea, and I always did myself when questioned; but I invariably found that those who laughed most in public were the first to make advances to me in private. I will not trouble you too much with the details of this period of my life."

"I am anxious, however, to know," said Justinian, "whether you brought your pet science seriously into play, and if so, whether with any satisfactory results."

"You must not press me too closely on that point," said John, "at present. I generally contrived to satisfy my clients; but on the whole I learnt perhaps as much as I taught. I have quick senses and a retentive memory, and, as I flatter myself, a happy knack of discovering other people's secrets without betraying too many of my own."

"I can say nothing against that statement," said Justinian; "but a man who sought information as to the future would hardly be contented by a recital of facts which he knew already, even though he might be astounded at your penetration."

"True," said John; "but given a certain craving for the marvellous, it is incredible how a man will accept as revelation, when put before him in a new light, facts which he has himself unconsciously revealed; and how eagerly, when thus prepared, he will gulp down an assurance of that which he desires, and mistake a shrewd guess at probabilities for actual prophecy."

"Your estimate of human intellect is not high," said Justinian, coldly. "I am to understand, then, that in all this you were never in earnest, and that your profession of a grand and mysterious science was merely a lure to attract dupes and obtain popularity?"

"And money," said John, coolly; "pray don't forget that. I could not afford to do anything gratis. But you mistake, sir. I took especial care to make no profession; on the contrary, when the belief in my powers began to spread, I did all I could to discourage it. Those who came to consult me found me most reluctant to oblige them with anything but legal advice."

"I see I must not play the critic too severely," said Justinian, smiling, in spite of himself, at John's imperturbable coolness and audacious sophistry. "Tell your story your own way."

"Had you been unlucky enough, sir," said John, "to know the majority of my clients, you would not have wondered at my holding them in small estimation, and scarcely worthy the expenditure of much scientific lore. Attracted by a vague report, they forced themselves upon me unsolicited ; they plagued me into pretending an interest in their contemptible fortunes, and they got as much or more than they expected—their money's worth. If any were dissatisfied I knew nothing of it. Possibly their fear of ridicule kept them silent ; possibly they still await the fulfilment of their destinies ; possibly I have a natural sense of the value of ambiguous expression, and in the old times might have done well in the oracular line. Be that as it may, when occasion required I could, and I can, be in earnest. I confess that I used those simpletons as stepping-stones to cross the ugly stream of poverty and obscurity. I crossed and never looked back. I wish I had nothing more serious to reproach myself with. It was hard work, too. I earned my money fairly. I have done as hard since and more unpleasant, but none that demanded greater tact and caution.

"I was about weary of the business when one day I had notice from a well-disposed young gentleman, to whom I had made a happy suggestion

about a marriage, that certain members of the
Court, having got wind of my reputation, had determined to pay me a visit in my character as astrologer; he gave me the probable hour and the names
of two of the party. You may imagine that in the
interim I was not idle.

" Sure enough they came, at a late hour, cloaked
and masked, and ripe for fun or mischief. This
time I resolved to be thoroughly in earnest; it was
an opportunity. There were four of them. By a
conspicuous ring, which he wears to this day—I
have a habit of noticing such marks of identity—I
recognized Hypatius, the nephew of Cæsar. What
passed is immaterial. I obtained all the data
necessary for my calculations. The party came
prepared to treat the matter as a jest, they went
away serious enough. But I was working for my
own satisfaction, not for theirs."

Here the Cappadocian paused. He could see
that the mention of Hypatius' name had fairly
roused the curiosity of Justinian. The face of the
latter, although he refrained from speaking, asked
the question plainly, " What of my rival ? "

" I discovered, sir," resumed John, answering
the mute inquiry—" I omit all the technicalities—
that at a certain time of life the Count was threatened with a great danger. The locality pointed to
as the source of the danger was the island of Venus
—Cyprus—and upon closer observation I was in-

duced to seek—again for my own satisfaction, for I have not had further communication with his Highness—to seek out one Acacius, a native of that island, whose peculiar occupation, as then keeper of the wild beasts, seemed also to be indicated by the conjunctions. Having made the acquaintance of this man I recommenced my inquiries upon fresh data, and with startling results. For the house of Acacius I found myself compelled to predict a splendid destiny."

"This is extraordinary," muttered Justinian.

"You at once perceive," continued John, "the significant connection between these two results, independently obtained; but the sequel is still more remarkable. Acacius was a man of great resolution and strength of character, with a temperament as fierce as that of one of his own tigers. Although but half educated, and holding a degrading office, he claimed to be descended from a very ancient stock—I believe royal—in his native island, and was inordinately proud of his pagan ancestors, still professing their religion. I need hardly tell you that he was to the last degree superstitious. It was not difficult to work upon such a character as this. He at once threw himself body and soul, with tigerish energy, upon the idea presented to him, and clung to it ferociously. And thus a man, upon whom no coercion would have had any effect, became my devoted slave.

" Unfortunately, as often happens in these cases, the data supplied to me were not sufficiently minute and accurate to build a perfect scheme upon, and after many attempts we were forced to rest contented with the vague assurance that before many years a grand destiny awaited the Cyprian's family, without being able to specify the individual member of it.

" At that time his family consisted of a son and three daughters. The boy was a model of strength and manly beauty, with a large share of his father's courage and resolution tempered by a fine intellect. Notwithstanding his origin, an enthusiast might be pardoned for regarding him with extravagant hope. Two years after, while assisting his father, he was killed by one of the lions. Despite his iron nerves, Acacius never got over the shock to his parental affection and to his ambition. I think he had pinned his faith on that boy—possibly I had myself —but he remained my staunch friend and assistant until within five years he, too, died, broken-hearted, in great poverty, dismissed and neglected by the Green Faction, on whom to the last he charged his death. With your permission, sir, I will not dwell over my own history during those years. It is sufficient to say that I served the government well, gained enormous experience, and was never suspected. I mention the last fact to prove to you the completeness of my confession. There is no other man in Constantinople who knows what my real calling was during that period."

"The secret service, of course," said Justinian mildly, his natural repugnance to the notion of an informer being almost neutralized by the dynamic presence of the Cappadocian. And, indeed, John was a rare study as he sat there recapitulating his varied experiences; every motion of his massive person, every line of his strong features, every glance of his aquiline eyes, and every tone of his richly modulated voice, suggesting indomitable energy and vitality. "I conclude, then," continued Justinian, "that your present honourable position was the reward of your service during the time you mention?"

"Not altogether. There again, sir, I must claim your indulgence. My first rise was, indeed, the reward of a very important service, but the latter was of such a nature that I shrink from confessing it until I have finished my narrative. It is not that I am deterred by regret or shame—I would act again in the same way under the same circumstances—but I dread disturbing the kindly equanimity with which you have listened to me. When you have heard me to the end you will take a broader view of my conduct and pass a mitigated judgment on that which you find especially displeasing. I promise then to answer any question."

"Your statement is voluntary," said Justinian; "follow your own plan."

"On his death-bed Acacius bequeathed to me a valuable legacy; he enabled me to fill his place in a secret society which had and still has great ends in view, and as a member of that society I won my second step by a yet bolder stroke. You remember, sir, that in the height of the popular excitement during the last riots, when the person of Cæsar was in imminent danger, he suddenly disappeared from the palace and for three days defied the vigilant search of his enemies. Had that search lasted for three years it would have been equally ineffectual. I had the good fortune to be the humble instrument in planning that escape and in finding a sanctuary for Cæsar."

"You!" exclaimed Justinian, utterly astonished. "You found a hiding-place for Cæsar!"

"I," replied John, in his fullest tones; "I, John the Cappadocian adventurer. To me Cæsar owes his liberty, and perhaps life. I saved him as I could save him again to-night, as I could save you were the whole Byzantine mob yelling for the blood of Justinian."

The steady, emphatic utterance of the Cappadocian was not that of a mere boaster, and Justinian knew it. After some thought he observed, "You have not been too liberally rewarded."

"The gratitude of princes," replied John, "must be limited by their power. Irregular and isolated services usually receive irregular rewards. Anas-

tasius is not one of those potent despots who can
venture to suddenly exalt an obscure individual to
high station. Under the circumstances I got as
much as I looked for. I have no grievance. I
hope never to have one. I never met a man possessed by such a thing who was worth anything."

"True. Conscious power has no time to expend
in grumbling," assented Justinian. "The secret
society you spoke of is, then, of considerable strength
and organization?"

"It has grand capabilities, which will develop
themselves when the proper moment arrives."

"It is fair to ask when that is likely to be?"

"I have authority to answer you," replied John
slowly, looking Justinian full in the face. "When
it becomes necessary to substitute the family of
Justin for that of Anastasius. That is the grand
cause to which we have pledged ourselves."

Justinian's heart gave a great leap when he heard
this candid declaration, and then for a moment his
whole being again shrank and narrowed under an
instinctive impulse of suspicion. After all, was it
not a trap? Who and what was this obscure
Cappadocian who talked so boldly of saving and
deposing Emperors—ex-informer and charlatan by
his own confession? And yet the idea of treachery
was absurd; it was too barefaced. Nor was it
possible that he, Justinian, could be classed with
simpletons, stepping-stones, and the like.

Meanwhile John waited quietly for him to speak.

"Is there no inconsistency," said Justinian at last, "between your loyal conduct at the time of the riots and this avowal, which, to speak plainly, amounts to pure treason?"

"None whatever," said John. "You must know yourself, sir, that had Anastasius been deposed or slain at that time, the Factions and the army would have opened the gates to Vitalian and made him master of the situation. I anticipated your charge of inconsistency. I have heard it before. If you will afford me another opportunity I will enter into this matter more fully; for the moment I prefer, with your leave, to complete my narrative."

"So be it," replied Justinian. "I am deeply interested."

"Acacius, then, left three daughters. With his last breath he exacted from me an oath that these children should appear as suppliants during the games at the Cynegium, and appeal to the pity of the Factions, or—and I believe this to have been uppermost in his mind—become a means of sowing discord between them. To the very last his ruling idea was for vengeance on the Greens. You remember what happened on the occasion when that oath was fulfilled?"

"I am not likely to forget it," said Justinian in his deep voice.

"Shortly afterwards Theodora and one of her

sisters, Comito, went upon the stage; the third, Anastasia, was taken charge of by the Lady Maria, now wife of Count Hypatius. I could do no more for them. At that time my resources were uncertain; I had not received my appointment. Five years of fruitless expectation had chilled my ardent hopes; there was no sign of success; the case seemed desperate. I could not afford to indulge any longer in the luxury of faith.

"A practical goal was necessary for my ambition. I had no fancy to be a mere unit in a Faction, struggling against absorption in chaotic turbulence, neither was I content to remain a salaried official, liable to be turned adrift at the first change in affairs. It was imperative that I should find a leader, to whose fortunes I might link my own; who might accept the offer of my energy, my experience, and my devotion. Long before this, sir, I had realized, in common with many thousands, that there was but one man who, although for the time being he held aloof from public affairs, could be accepted as the man of the future. Yourself! Your Illustrious uncle Justin might be the foundation, but you would become the perfect edifice. It was then that I began to watch you closely, in the presumptuous hope of detecting some loophole in your fortress by which to gain admittance. That I was successful is scarcely remarkable; it is but an llustration of the old truth that human patience is all-effectual. But that in following up my new venture I should have come across the clue which I had abandoned in despair, that the existences of Justinian and the daughter of Acacius should be found inclining towards each other—in however infinitesimal a degree, still inclining—is a fact which leads us into a field of conjecture immeasurably vast, where the sonorous dicta of man's experience and philosophy sound like the vapid prattle of a child."

The Cappadocian again ceased speaking. His tone during the concluding sentences had been replete with solemnity and conviction. There was silence for a while, and then Justinian began, with a tinge of sadness in his grave voice.

"This is a subject on which for the present I cannot trust myself to speak. It requires deep consideration. I see some points in a new light, some I see now for the first time. There are riddles of life which all human learning and research are impotent to solve, which demonstrate the utter grossness and weakness of mortal capacity. My mind is disturbed. It is my habit on such occasions to devote some hours to private meditation, and to seeking higher counsel than man can give. I thank you for your candid and interesting narrative, and the complimentary offer of your services; I fully recognize their value, but to approve or disapprove, to accept or refuse, to form

any immediate judgment, would be unfair both on
you and on myself. If you will favour me with an
interview at the same time to-morrow I shall be
better prepared. I will not even ask you now what
was the nature of the service which gained your first
promotion, and which you were so reluctant to
confess—I reserve the right of demanding an explanation when I think fit. I have your promise?".

"Undoubtedly," said John, rising; "at any
moment I am ready to redeem it." But in his
heart he was galled at this sudden lack of interest.
"And now, sir, I will take my leave."

Justinian, resting his head upon his hand, was
plunged in deep thought. "Stay," he said, abruptly, "I will ask one more question. "Can you
tell me by whose orders my messenger was waylaid?"

"By the Lady Lupicina's," replied John.

Justinian started. "You are certain of this?"

"Certain."

Justinian mused again, and a stern, almost
savage, expression settled upon his face. He
stretched out his hand and took up the letter.
"To-morrow," he said, "you shall read this. I
will send it in spite of every one if you will undertake to be the bearer."

"I am at your service," said John, "but I beg
of you, sir, to consider the matter thoroughly before
you act."

"Be sure I shall do so," said Justinian, haughtily. "It is my habit. I have the whole night before me for reflection. I can do without sleep."

"I wish I could say the same," said John. "It is living two lives in one."

"With double care and double responsibility."

"And double gain," added the Cappadocian, bowing himself out. "He is love-sick again," he soliloquized, as he passed down the corridors. "The name of Theodora is enough. He will never be the man he can be until this matter is settled one way or the other." And John made his way into the street, somewhat disturbed by the idea of running against the Lady Lupicina. But that formidable person was engaged elsewhere, as we shall see in another chapter.

CHAPTER VI.

LAIS AND CORNELIA.

IT was after sunset. The lamps were lighted in
Theodora's apartments—lamps of agate, sardonyx,
and cornelian, gold-mounted, begemmed, and fed
with perfumed oil, steeping their luxurious surroundings in a soft mellow glow, and filling
the air with a delicate fragrance. The delicious
interior was to the last degree suggestive of its
occupant—of reckless extravagance, voluptuous
excess, artistic feeling, feminine refinement, and
eccentric taste, all strangely blended in a single
character. On one panel glowed a mythological
fresco more than warm in subject and treatment;
against another hung a broad blade, notched and
iron-hafted, or a sheaf of venomous-looking arrows.
Here stood a tinted statuette of a bacchante,
modelled from Theodora herself; there a single
perfect blossom, in a glass vase of chaste simplicity.
The fair dancer, wrapped in a dressing-robe, snow-

white, pearl-embroidered, lay upon a couch, half dozing, half lost in dreamy fancies ; and on a table beside her were placed the last offerings of Ecebolus —an enamelled model of a racing chariot and team of horses ready for the start, and a miniature of himself exquisitely painted on ivory.

It was settled at last. Chrysomalla was about to lose her lodger. As that far-seeing woman prophesied, the young Tyrian proved irresistible in the end, and Theodora had consented to take possession of the splendid residence he had prepared for her. The gossips of Constantinople darted about like bluebottles, buzzing with tales of the lavish luxury of this new abode, and jeering at, denouncing, or envying the sin and folly of the donor. We will not dwell upon the picture of Theodora's rapid demoralization—hideously rapid, despite her frequent bursts of better feeling, her impulses of charity, and generous actions. To analyze the degradation of a noble nature, especially in a woman, is not a pleasant task. She had attained the fearful pre-eminence which she herself foretold. She had become the Queen of Iniquity.

By most women in her position, and by a good many out of it, the splendid prospect before her would have been contemplated with rapture. But it was otherwise with Theodora. She had grown so enamoured of the unchecked freedom of her professional life, checked only by her engagements with the theatre, where at each appearance she gained a fresh triumph, and attracted a fresh crowd of devotees to her unhallowed shrine, that even the frail ties which were to unite her to Ecebolus—frail enough they were, in all conscience —galled her in imagination.

She had stipulated that she was to be under no kind of restraint, and even to this condition the infatuated young man consented, trusting blindly to his personal influence and fascinations to create some sort of future control. As to leaving the stage, that she would not hear of, even if her engagement could be cancelled. The delirium of success was too sweet to be resigned. Perhaps, too, she was conscious that her unapproachable superiority in her own line redeemed her from being altogether contemptible as well as vile. It was noticeable, however, that her dancing had lost in a great degree that subtle chasteness of motion which had made even Justinian and Belisarius forget the revelation of the woman in the consummate skill and delicacy of the artist.

Nevertheless, the idea of this nominal yoke distressed her, and yet she had consented to it. How could she do otherwise ? How forego so glorious a revenge upon society ?—upon that society which condemned her and the like of her as outcasts, and idolized them only while they remained such ; which shuddered at their iniquity and gloated over it, grudging them repentance and reformation; which said, "They are the vilest of things, but they are the most delightful. Their lot in the next world is eternal perdition, but in this they entertain us. We cannot afford to lose *our* entertainment; let *them* be lost!" Moreover, if all that was meet and wholesome in her womanhood was deadened or distorted, she was still a very woman, and no fabled god ever descended upon earth in shape more glorious than that of Ecebolus.

But, in reality, even the savage consciousness of wrong and shame, which was in itself a sign of better things, was passing away. She had ceased to torment herself with scruples and remorse, or fits of bitter indignation. With all the passionate intensity of her nature she revelled in fervid draughts of that goblet the first compulsory taste of which had been so odious. Was the odium, in truth, for the taste or the compulsion?

In person she was more lovely than ever, and her loveliness of that kind which never becomes sensualized or marred. She was an exquisite fraud. Her face, contrasted with her career, was an anomaly, like the figure of Chastity graven on a gem which decks the painted bosom of a harlot. But the gem may still find a virgin resting-place such as the engraver designed it for, and the Divine Artist who moulded the clay knew that it would one day be tenanted by a chastened and purified soul.

Now as she reclined on the couch, breathing peacefully, her eyes closed with the long lashes sweeping down on her pure cheek, her glorious chestnut tresses spread over the pillow, and her hands crossed upon her bosom, she looked like some sweet saint musing on beatific visions rather than a miserable sinner devising fresh sinfulness.

There came a sharp rap at the door, and without waiting for the usual permission, a smart handmaid entered hurriedly, looking scared and perplexed.

Theodora languidly opened her eyes. "Who is there? Is it you, Glycystoma? Why do you disturb me?"

"Madam, there is a woman—a person—it is very tall; she might be a man in disguise."

"Nonsense!" said Theodora, pettishly. "Say I am tired, asleep, out,—say what you please. I cannot see any one. Only go, and leave me quiet."

"I have said all that, madam, and more besides. She will take no denial; she will come in. Oh!"

What more the girl might have added will never be known; for with a little shriek she suddenly disappeared backwards through the doorway, as though plucked from behind, and in her place a tall, angular, and indifferently female figure presented itself, shrouded in sombre drapery, with a hood concealing the face.

"Leave us," said this apparition, in a stern,

harsh tone, addressing the maid. But Glycystoma stood her ground boldly.

"Am I to go, madam?" she asked her mistress, "or shall I call for assistance? If you are afraid, I——"

Theodora had half raised herself from the couch, and sat regarding her visitor with a mixture of curiosity and annoyance. "Afraid, child!" she said; "you know I am never afraid. You can go and wait at the end of the passage." Then she sat up. "Perhaps you will explain this intrusion. Who are you?"

The apparition deliberately assured itself that the door was fast, and advancing to the centre of the room threw back her hood, and replied—

"I am Lupicina, the aunt of Justinian, and I have come to see the woman who has bewitched him."

There was no one in Constantinople but was familiar with the fame of the Lady Lupicina, the austere wife of Justin, and few to whom her masculine features were unknown. And now Theodora found herself, in her own house, face to face with this grim dame, whom as a child she had frequently contemplated with awe. That she, of all people in the world, should visit her!

"Lupicina! The Lady Lupicina!" she exclaimed, so utterly taken aback by the announcement of her visitor's name that the close of the speech passed for the moment unheeded. But for all her amazement she rose from the couch and gracefully glided to place a chair for the great lady. " May I beg of you to be seated, madam ? " she said, softly.

" Do you think it likely I will sit down in this house ? " retorted Lupicina. " Stand out there that I may look at you, if you are not ashamed, and if this meretricious light will let me. I suppose it serves to hide the paint and false hair. Faugh ! the smell of this place is stifling."

" If the perfumes annoy you, madam, I can throw back the lattice," said Theodora. Now that the first surprise was over, she began to enjoy the novelty of the situation, and felt singularly free from irritation or embarrassment.

" No," said Lupicina, roughly. " I shall not faint. Let me see you."

" Certainly, madam," said Theodora, drawing herself up ; and raising her hand, she removed the shade from the lamp above her. Her loose sleeve fell back to the shoulder, leaving bare her arm— round as a sapling, white and polished as the halcyon's egg ; her robe, slightly girded at the waist, indicated her graceful form, her bright tresses rippled down to her ankles, and the light which fell from above on her perfect features marked the slight furrow between her brows, and lent intensity to the dark, steady orbs beneath.

In her turn Lupicina was amazed. She had not dreamt of seraphic loveliness like this. For some moments sheer wonder kept her silent. Then she said—

"Ay, ay, you have the curse of beauty. To do you justice, you show more like an angel than a—— " But with that vision before her even her unsparing lips refused to complete the sentence.

Theodora completed it for her. "A devil," she added quietly. "Why not say it, madam? This is scarcely a visit of ceremony."

"And if I did say it," exclaimed Lupicina, with sudden fierceness, "who shall gainsay me? Have you not blighted the rich harvest that I have sown and tended, when it was full and ripe? Who but a devil incarnate could undo the patient training of a lifetime—could seduce the most stainless and virgin soul that ever was in man—could poison with her own image a mind devoted to lofty thoughts and glorious aims?"

"A fair woman might effect all that, madam," said Theodora, with calm emphasis on the potential. "People tell me I am one, and many add that I am a devil; but in neither character can I accuse myself of the particular havoc you describe. I have had no experience of stainless and virgin souls."

"Are there not in this city," continued Lupicina, "libertines and fools enough to minister to your

profligacy and extravagance? Is it not enough
that you have spread your toils for that hapless
young Tyrian, and ensnared him body and soul;
but that he, too, must be entangled in the accursed
meshes whom God has marked out for a ruler of
men and a pillar of righteousness?"

"I fear I shall have but little chance in that
case," replied ·Theodora ironically, as if suggesting
sounder views of the doctrine of election.

"But, by the Mother of God, I will baffle you!"
thundered Lupicina, lashing herself into a fury.
"What are you, that you should work this evil?
You may be an angel in form, but you are
possessed by a legion of devils. I have power;
for all your beauty I will have you scourged like
a dog, and driven howling from the city. You
shall be cast out in this world as you are cast out
to all eternity."

"This is madness, madam, and unworthy of
you," interrupted Theodora, with dignity. "I have
not the faintest notion with what object you have
forced your way into my house and attacked me
thus violently. But you *are* in my house. You
are a great lady, whom all Constantinople respects;
I am a dancer—but you are my guest; you have
made yourself so. I cannot answer your invective.
I implore you to consider our respective positions.
I am not afraid of your threats, but if you will
condescend to explain your meaning quietly, I will

do my best to satisfy you. There must be some extraordinary mistake."

"There is none," cried Lupicina, savagely. "Where is the letter you have received from my nephew, Justinian?"

Theodora opened her great eyes to their widest. "A letter—to me—from your nephew, Justinian!" she repeated, slowly. "Oh, madam, you are not in earnest, or some one has cruelly imposed upon you. What possible reason could the noble Justinian have for writing to me?"

"Reason!" said Lupicina, sneering ferociously. "A reason you know well. The fine reason that every man has when he is stricken with madness, and is ready to sacrifice his prospects in life and his hopes of salvation to his passion for a worthless woman."

"Oh, that is it?" remarked Theodora. "I thank you for the information, madam; this is the first I have heard of it."

"It is a lie," said Lupicina, coarsely.

"It is no lie," replied the dancer, feeling miraculously temperate and collected. "I perceive that virtue and piety are apparently incompatible with common courtesy. I swear to you that if your incredible statement about your nephew's passion for me be correct, I learn it now for the first time from the lips of his aunt."

Then poor Lupicina realized the position. I ask

your pity for her. The grim old Dacian was no tactician. Setting to work in her fierce, rugged, barbarian fashion, her efforts to save her idol from destruction had resulted in a second blunder more fatal than the first. She had confessed his passion for a woman to the woman herself.

"What have I done—what have I done?" groaned the wretched lady, clasping her hands.

At the bottom of her heart Theodora was sorry for her, at the same time she had a strong inclination to burst out laughing. Throughout the interview she, as a rule so quick-tempered, had never felt seriously annoyed by Lupicina's insulting language, having suspected that the whole thing was some huge mistake. Of course it was not pleasant to be called hard names, or to be threatened with scourging and the like, but it was notorious throughout Constantinople that, with all her good qualities, the Lady Lupicina was only two-thirds civilized, and that even in court circles she would occasionally launch out, regardless of all etiquette, in a way that made the fine ladies quiver with terror or indignation. Besides, the special charge against Theodora was to her so utterly groundless and absurd, that for once she experienced the sensation of being an injured innocent. Justinian, forsooth— why, she did not know him by sight! Ah, yes, he was once pointed out to her at the theatre—a grave, plain man, with a bald forehead, round eyes,

and a rather red face ; a man who was steeped
up to his eyes in learning, who never touched
wine and hated women, whom some people spoke
of as likely to be Emperor one of these days.
And he in love with her! What a monstrous
absurdity !

And now Lupicina's sudden recognition of her
egregious blunder, and consequent collapse, so
tickled Theodora's sense of humour, that had not
the anguish of the grey-haired dame been unmistakably genuine, she would certainly have betrayed
her amusement. But she said gently—

" Do not distress yourself, madam ; there is no
harm done. My toils would be powerless against
your noble quarry, even if I had any desire to
spread them in that direction, which, believe me,
I have not. Besides, as you have said, they are
already full."

Lupicina's harsh features grew more composed
as the girl's melodious voice uttered this comforting
speech, and out of her growing thankfulness at the
possible rescue of Justinian, she could afford a
crumb or two of courtesy to the fair sinner before
her ; she actually growled a kind of apology.
Perhaps she had spoken too strongly. She had
been terribly anxious of late, and so forth, ending
with a sort of compromise between a curse and a
compliment.

" Unhappy girl ! you might, indeed, come between

a saint and his God. Woe, that so fair a body should be devoted to the service of Satan!"

"Erotic saintliness is not to my taste," retorted Theodora, maliciously, "and hypocrisy the one, perhaps the only, vice which I detest."

Lupicina winced, but she knew not how to reply to this thrust at her frail idol. The position of the two women was being curiously reversed. In her own sphere Lupicina was accounted irresistible, a kind of female Achilles; but now Theodora, by sheer force of character, began to overrule the aggressive righteousness of her turbulent adversary.

"If what you assert be true——" said Lupicina.

"*If,* madam!" interrupted Theodora. "Why *if?* What do you suppose to be my object in deceiving you? Do you imagine I desire the conquest of your nephew, when I have conquered that?" and laughing scornfully she pointed to the minature of Ecebolus.

A flippant, arrogant speech; but it told as Theodora intended it should. Lupicina winced again. With inconsistency truly feminine her pride in Justinian was bitterly mortified by these taunts which ought merely to have assured her of his perfect safety. The hack-and-hew style of her attack was impotent against the cunning fence of her despised adversary. She was soon discomfited by unexpected resistance, and could not do justice to herself. It was even easier work to plan an outrage with Barsumas than to bandy words with this audacious dancer. Theodora was unwittingly avenging Belisarius.

But one source never failed to supply Lupicina with an answer; had she always turned to that she had fared better. She glanced towards the miniature, and in solemn, rolling accents quoted'the tremendous words —

" 'He goeth after her straightway as an ox goeth to the slaughter, or as a fool to the correction of the stocks; till a dart strike through his liver; as a bird hasteth to the snare, and knoweth not that it is for his life. . . . She hath cast down many wounded: yea, many strong men have been slain by her. Her house is the way to hell, going down to the chambers of death.' "

For an instant Theodora bowed her stubborn head. The last despairing stroke of Lupicina's ponderous, two-handed falchion smote even through her armour of wickedness and stunned her. Her defiant eyes dropped, and the thought-furrow between them deepened to a strong line, but she quickly recovered herself and looked up boldly, to see Lupicina watching her with a stern yet compassionate gaze.

"They are not my words—they are not my words!" cried the old lady; "if in any degree they touch you, for the love of Christ harden not your heart against them. I regret much that I have said.

Something tells me, now that I have seen you, that with fairer treatment—— But you will reject my pity, as you would reject any bribe I could offer you. I understand you so far. The mystery of your guilty life is one of the secrets of Omniscience; man has no choice but unsparing condemnation. But I came here to-night neither to preach nor to condemn, simply to save my son. To that I have been ready to sacrifice everything and everybody; for that, sinner that I am, I have been ready to endanger my own soul. I have only lately consented—God help me!—to a base, unworthy act, for which I shall do penance to my life's end; but it was to save him. If you will work with me in this, will help me to save him from himself, you will be doing that which, by the mercy of God, may atone for much evil, and which I believe you will never repent. I do not seek to bribe you, but if you will help me now, the day may come when I can repay the service. As God hears me, if I am alive and if my duty as a Christian will permit, I will do so. In the day of your trouble, which must come, which comes to us all, I will remember you. Great as is the gulf between us, I will cross it then to your assistance, as I have now for my own ends. And I pray, and will ever pray, to the holy saints to bring you to repentance, and to intercede to save you from eternal death. Only help me—help me to save my son!"

Yes, between these women there was verily a great gulf, as great as that between heaven and hell. They were as opposite and as far asunder as the poles, but nevertheless they had come to a kind of understanding, and their contest had resulted in at least mitigated antagonism. Lupicina had expected to find Theodora beautiful, but in a coarser and more animal style, with expression, manners, and voice to correspond, exciting loathing and contempt. She had not the shrewdness of John of Cappadocia, to guess at the true nature of Justinian's passion. Ascribing it herself to direct infernal agency, she could only picture the object of it as infernal, even in her charms, and paid her nephew the compliment of supposing him to be enamoured of a gross female fiend.

Now, in spite of her natural and educational abhorrence of the dancer, she was forced to admit that, personally, Theodora was neither abominable nor contemptible, not without traces of that which might once have been, or might have become, a noble character. Faint praise, truly; but a great concession from one of the female elect of those, or possibly any, times. If the close of her speech betrayed an overconsciousness of her condescension in stooping to touch pitch, it enhanced her offer of risking the defilement a second time, and Theodora was able to detect in her turn that Lupicina was not so hardened in righteousness that her bowels of compassion had undergone complete ossification. The wintry gleam of kindliness made the dancer relax ever so slightly the strict folds of that impenetrable cloak of sin which, under the pelting storm of wrath and denunciation, she had drawn tighter round her.

"I will do all in my power," said Theodora, "to assist you; but are you not overrating the danger?"

"No, no," said Lupicina; "no, I know him so well. He is slow in deciding, but his decisions are unalterable. He has written to you—he will write again. I cannot tell when this temptation first came upon him, but he could not long conceal it from me as he has from others. I watched him fighting against it, half yielding, and then fighting again. I prayed day and night to the saints to give him the victory. Then I saw that he had come to a determination, and I watched the more, and set others to watch. Were he hasty and impulsive, I should be less terrified; but he is so deliberate in his resolutions. He has written to you—he has written to you, I say; where is the letter?"

"If I might ask for more details," said Theodora, "it would be possible to conjecture, but at present—— "

"You shall know everything," interrupted Lupicina, "and you will help me as you have promised. Tell me, was there a young man brought into this house two days ago senseless and wounded?"

"Not into these apartments, but into Chrysomalla's. This is her house. I was not at home when it happened, but I have heard all about it. It was the splendid young Thracian who saved Antonina, Demas's daughter, from drowning. He was waylaid in the street."

"He was the bearer of the letter," said Lupicina.

"Are you quite sure of that?"

"Quite sure. He is in my nephew's service."

"Chrysomalla and the girls attended to him and brought him round, but they spoke of no letter for me or any one. It was probably stolen from him when he was senseless."

"No," said Lupicina, "it was not, or I should have got it myself. He would not give it up; he is strong as Samson." She stopped short, seeing she had committed herself, and then went on with fierce energy. "Yes, it was my doing! For my son's sake I consented to a grievous wrong—to the attack on that noble youth. I hoped that you would have gone to him"—pointing to the miniature of Ecebolus—"before the letter was sent. But the tempter was too quick with his suggestions. Then I tried to intercept it—vainly, as you know; it could not be wrested from the bearer without bloodshed, and that—that was forbidden."

"The line was drawn rather finely," thought

Theodora; but she merely observed, "I did hear that the young man was rescued. Do his assailants know by whom?"

"No; by a band of men, strangers, of the Green Faction, who happened to arrive at the critical moment. They carried the Thracian insensible into this house, and were seen to leave it shortly afterwards. The letter must have been in his possession then. Who has taken it?"

"I think," said Theodora, "that if directed to me, it would have been delivered. When the poor boy came to his senses he was no doubt still half stunned, and forgot it."

"He is too trustworthy," said Lupicina. "He could cling to it as long as there was life in him; he would have tried to deliver it at his last gasp, if it had not been taken from him."

"Is it not rather strange," mused Theodora, "that the rescuers should have deposited the Thracian here, and have taken their departure so suddenly, and since then should neither have come forward to make inquiries nor to claim a reward?"

"They might have their reasons for avoiding publicity, or they might require no reward for an act of common humanity."

"They might have taken the letter," suggested Theodora.

"Good God!" exclaimed Lupicina; "then into whose hands has it fallen?"

"Do not agitate yourself, madam," said Theodora. "If you will excuse me, I will leave you for a short time, and make some inquiries of Chrysomalla's household. They know it is worth their while to tell me the truth. You will be quite safe from intrusion here;" and she glided from the room.

Left alone, Lupicina recovered her equanimity, and began with grim curiosity to survey the apartment. Fortunately, the subdued light barely illuminated those decorations and works of art which might have provoked another explosion of her wrath; and her eyes were again attracted by the miniature of Ecebolus. She went nearer to examine it.

"He, too," she murmured to herself, "so young, so glorious in his beauty—he, too, is ensnared and must perish! There is nothing depraved or licentious in that face; there should be noble capabilities beneath that clear, well-shaped brow; with all its womanish beauty, the mouth is firm and eloquent. Can Heaven permit these triumphs of iniquity? Is she not a scourge sent upon this profligate city to hasten its condemnation? Is she not Dæmonodora?"

But the dancer soon returned, and the thoughts of Lupicina reverted to her one great subject of anxiety.

"I think, madam," said Theodora, "that I can throw some light on this matter; but I warn you, if my suspicions are correct, you may consider the obvious conclusions not reassuring. It appears that two nights ago there was a visitor in Chrysomalla's apartments, who left the house just about the time when the Thracian was attacked. He is known as John of Cappadocia, a lawyer, and now Prætorian secretary. In former days I knew him personally—a crafty, dangerous man, ready to turn his hand to anything which is profitable. In his employ there is one Isidore, an ex-chorister, who has frequently been seen with him, here and elsewhere. It was this man Isidore who roused the household and assisted in carrying in the young Thracian. We may therefore safely conclude that he and his master represent the band who frightened your agents and effected the rescue, either by accident or design. Moreover, I am told that the first act of the messenger on coming to his senses was to feel anxiously in the breast of his tunic, and that he appeared much startled and distressed at missing something. The letter was there, madam, when your agents could not wrest it from him; it was not there when he felt for it. It had disappeared in the interval. It was either lost in bringing him in, or it was taken from him by John the Cappadocian, who in that case will use it to serve his own purposes. Had it been dropped in the street, be sure it would have been delivered to me either here or at the theatre—I have the character of being liberal—supposing it to have been directed."

"It *was* directed," said Lupicina. "When I met Belisarius in the corridor, coming out of his master's room, he was reading the direction. But there was something else besides the letter—that he thrust hastily into his bosom; there was a small packet in his other hand, and my son has been watched in the shop of Alexander the jeweller."

Theodora's lip curled. "Rest assured, then," she said, "that both are in the possession of the Cappadocian. The point is what use he will make of them. If you can discover that he is in communication with your nephew, that will be decisive. He will be making overtures of some kind to him. If not, he will possibly try to renew his acquaintance with me. In either case he is certain to rely upon the letter which he has stolen."

"We are undone!" groaned Lupicina. "Such a man will glory in proclaiming our shame to the world."

"I think not. The Cappadocian is crafty and unscrupulous, but not malicious. He is far more likely to try and curry favour with your nephew by becoming his—his—accomplice."

Lupicina winced again at the ugly word.

"Supposing, then, that the letter eventually reaches me, and that its contents are such as you suppose, which to me appears incredible, I shall be glad of your instructions how to act."

" You will promise me," said Lupicina, after some thought, " that whatever proposals are made to you by my son, or on his behalf, either by letter or otherwise, you will reject them absolutely and unconditionally."

" Most willingly," said Theodora, with some scornful emphasis ; " the promise does not involve much self-denial."

To her nature, open, frank, and defiant, even in its guilt, there was something repulsive in this reptile, stealthy passion of Justinian.

" Will you swear it ? " asked Lupicina hesitatingly, with some doubt as to the value of a dancer's oath.

" I swear it," answered Theodora, " and by the memory of my father." Her solemn, lowered tone satisfied even her sceptical companion.

" I must also implore you," continued Lupicina, almost humbly, " to make your rejection so hopeless, so galling and distasteful to him, that he will never seek to renew his proposals ; and this will not be easy. Do you understand me ? "

" Partially," said Theodora, getting more and more astonished. " You wish me to disgust him. I can do so easily. But he is hardly likely to be so persistent as to require it."

" Girl ! " exclaimed Lupicina, stamping her foot, " why do you argue with me ? You do not know him. I do. Persistency is the great feature of his character—patient, inflexible determination. Do you think he has entered lightly upon this falsification of his whole life? I tell you no thought of woman, much less of woman polluted, degraded, and—— "

"Ah! madam," interposed Theodora, "spare me any further invective. We have done with that, and it is wasted upon me."

" Until your image possessed it," said Lupicina, less excitedly, " his was a maiden soul. If he is thus false to himself it is because the arch-tempter, who always studies the idiosyncrasy of his victims, has been permitted to fill his mind with specious arguments, which he will have duly weighed and considered."

" Once for all, then, I am prepared to do all you require of me as thoroughly as I can, if the opportunity presents itself," said Theodora, again smitten with an unseasonable sense of the humorous. For the life of her she could not take a serious view of the stealthy proceedings of this studious, religious, methodical, not too good looking or too juvenile admirer, whom she had scarcely seen and never met face to face. His passion! Pshaw! the superstitious anxiety of Lupicina bordered upon insanity. What if the whole affair were the creation of a morbid fancy? The Thracian might have been going to fifty places on his master's business when he was attacked, poor boy, by Lupicina's ruffians;

and the whole sequel might be easily explained as accidental coincidence. She had given her promise, and now the sooner the interview ended the better. Lupicina was becoming somewhat wearisome over her immaculately wayward nephew.

" He is proud and sensitive," continued that lady, volunteering further information, " and has a noble recognition of his own worth. How can he fail to have it, when his superiority to other men is so marked ? "

" Thank you," said Theodora, indifferently. " I shall know how to act."

" He will always accept counsel and advice, but interference with his plans only confirms him in his resolution. He will hate me at first," added Lupicina, sorrowfully, " if he discover the part I have played in the matter, but the time may come when he will be grateful."

" There is no absolute reason that he should know anything about it, madam," said Theodora, charitably interpreting this last hint, " if you keep your own counsel. I will not betray you, if I can help it."

And now Lupicina's mind seemed to be somewhat relieved. " I need not intrude upon you longer," she said, " nor need I repeat what I have said. If I live I will repay your promised service. And now God grant that, in helping to save this one soul, you are covering a multitude of sins.

Farewell." And she moved with stately step towards the door. There she turned and looked again at Theodora. With a sudden burst of real feeling, she cried aloud, "Poor child! repent, repent! For the love of Christ, repent before it is too late!" and bowing her head, passed sorrowfully out.

When Lupicina reached home, she sent for Barsumas. Her first inquiry was, "Has any one been with my son?"

"John the Cappadocian, Prætorian secretary, has been closeted with his Nobility for a considerable time," said Barsumas; "he has only just left the house."

"She was right," said Lupicina to herself, "it was well I went. I have saved him."

Out of all that was said during the interview, Theodora cared to remember little except her own promise; but at intervals through the night, ay, and for long afterwards, her unwilling, rebellious ears retained the ring of that awful sentence—

"Her house is the way to hell, going down to the chambers of death."

CHAPTER VII.

JUSTINIAN'S LETTER.

AMONG the various missives which Theodora received the following morning was a small note, carefully sealed and without signature, containing these words : "You were right. Last night, whilst I was with you, he was here. Be ready and remember." It had been left, so said the girl who delivered it, very early, by a horrid-looking fat man.

And in the afternoon another special visitor was announced whilst Theodora sat alone expecting Ecebolus. It was John of Cappadocia. She knew, of course, the object of his visit. It had come rather sooner than she anticipated, that was all. To receive him she went into a side room, where they would not be interrupted.

John entered, with his usual self-possessed and imperturbable air. At the sight of him Theodora felt a slight twinge of disagreeable emotion. He was connected with some of the most disagreeable passages in her life; the death-bed of her father, the brutal visit of her stepmother, and her appearance as suppliant in the Cynegium. And behind these, again, there was a retrospect of youthful experiences in which he figured conspicuously, and seldom to advantage. She could not in her heart allege against him any definite accusation. He had possessed some mysterious hold over her father, who, during the last years of his life, had been devoted to him; he had always shown a fair amount of kindness to herself and her sisters, and when their troubles came upon them had behaved quite as generously, perhaps more so, than could have been expected of a struggling advocate; he had accurately carried out their father's dying injunctions; but through all this his presence had invariably excited in her a certain amount of antipathy for which in other days she had often taken herself seriously to task. And now when they met again, after a very long interval, and under entirely different circumstances, she felt the same. It was in no way connected with her knowledge, imperfect as that was, of his adventurer's career, of his unscrupulousness and want of principle. Of all people she could least afford to be intolerant and hypercritical. The antipathy was purely personal, that of one individual for the other; inexplicable and apparently causeless, but actual all the same.

Was it not the intuitive animosity, which certain natures have, to others compounded of attributes the most antithetical and repugnant to their own, which is quite independent of ethical and social contingencies, and to a certain extent brutish— which the dog has to the fox, the rat, the weasel, and all kinds of vermin; the stag to the sheep; which a poor sempstress may have to some fine-lady customer; a curate to a bishop, a son to his father, and a father to his son?

But Theodora's depression had passed away with the night; she felt in high spirits, and anticipated with mischievous satisfaction the coming passage of arms. Accordingly she greeted John with much affability, without any allusion to the long gap in their acquaintance, as though for months past he had been in the habit of looking in occasionally on her as well as on her neighbour.

The Cappadocian, with a full appreciation of Theodora's tact, was not slow in taking his cue. Such lives as theirs had no business with by-gones. The pleasures of memory represent a very fluctuating and conditional fund of enjoyment. And thus their discourse flowed easily and pleasantly for some time; but in John's demeanour there was a certain gravity, as of a man weighted with an important negotiation.

"Then you intend to leave these apartments almost directly?" he said.

"I shall remain three or four days longer at the most," replied Theodora, suspecting that the real fun was about to begin.

"Your mind is quite made up?" said John, after a pause.

"Quite."

"Nothing could induce you to change it?"

"Well, no, I think not; nothing that I can imagine. Why do you ask?"

"There might be inducements which you cannot imagine," said John, solemnly.

Theodora felt excessively vivacious. A playfully bold idea suggested itself to her. "I can startle him out of this nonsensical gravity," she thought to herself. "The thing is ridiculous from beginning to end. If I am mistaken in my guess, what does it matter? I will risk it." And she answered, "I have a strong imagination too. I can picture to myself several things which might occur."

"As for instance?" drawled John, leaning back and surveying her.

"As for instance, that, after the proper introductory remarks, his Excellency the Prætorian secretary might present me with a letter, and possibly something else."

John's trained countenance never changed; not the faintest movement of eyelid or lip betrayed his surprise. And yet it was great. "How can she know," he thought, "who is at the bottom of this? The Thracian let out nothing. Who, then?" and even while he continued speaking, his mind took a rapid survey of the novel position in the game, and he half regretted having thought it unnecessary to keep Isidore on the watch near Chrysomalla's house. The fact was that it would have required a whole corps of Isidores to carry out the Cappadocian's system to perfection. "As you are prepared," he said calmly, "it makes my part the simpler. Here is the letter, and—the something else. Is it any use asking how you came to know this?"

"I am a sorceress," said Theodora, admiring his perfect coolness, but suddenly afraid that she might have endangered Lupicina's secret. If this crafty man once guessed that some one had been beforehand with him, he would never rest until he discovered who. Well, the old savage must take her chance like other people.

"You have indeed a habit of enchanting," said John, rather ponderously, "but the range of your spells is probably greater than even you can divine."

"Scarcely," said Theodora, in a clear, high key. "I know my own powers. I can bewitch one as well as another. Sage as well as fool, saint as well as sinner, pedant as well as profligate, Timon as well as Alcibiades."

"Hem! you know who is the writer of this?" asked John, feeling sure she did.

Theodora laughed. "The last man in the world who ought to have written it. How long have you taken to this trade?" she added.

Her tone was bitterly contemptuous, but John regarded her with complacent admiration. He felt a sort of proprietary pride in this exquisite argosy which he had launched upon the perilous waves, and was now endeavouring to pilot into a haven of safety and repose.

"That trade being?"

"That of—of"—she hesitated significantly for a word—"that of go-between in affairs of this nature."

"This is my first essay as ambassador," returned John, placidly.

"Ambassador!" sneered Theodora, tossing her beautiful head. "The word is grand."

"And yet not unsuitable to the occasion, as you will confess when you have read this." And John handed her the letter.

"You persist, then, in carrying the farce through? Why need I read that? It is almost a pity to break the seal. I can write my answer on the outside; an immense 'No.'"

"And afterwards suffer the agonies of unsatisfied curiosity. Spare yourself, and accept this."

She took the letter petulantly. "I imagined you

to be a shrewd, clear-sighted man of the world," she said, becoming ruder as she became more irritated by John's imperturbability. "Do you now, knowing as much of me as you do, as all the world knows—do you seriously believe that I will listen for one instant to this absurd proposal ? "

"Do not excite yourself needlessly. Permit me to remark that you have no knowledge of its nature."

"Bah ! I can guess. The old story in some new guise. It never really varies. Possibly a little less frankness than usual, a spice of hypocritical sentiment, choicer expressions, and in the end—the old story. Whatever it be, I repeat my question, do you seriously think I will listen to it ?"

"No," replied John; "I seriously believe that you will not. I said as much when I undertook to be the bearer of it, and I say it again now."

The answer was disconcerting. Even supposing that she had the least inclination to waver, she was tied by her oath to one ultimate decision. She had looked to relieving the tameness of the whole affair by taking the high moral tone, and treating John to a gush of sarcastic indignation, to expressing her opinion freely concerning both agent and principal. And now this amiable resolve was partially neutralized. The Cappadocian was her master. As Theodora had avenged Belisarius overnight, so was John now avenging Lupicina.

" Then why on earth did you take the trouble of bringing it ?" she exclaimed pettishly.

" For the sake of the writer. Some diseases are best cured by excision. Your answer will be the operating knife. It is easier to heal a raw wound than an insidious cancer."

" Indeed ! A nice predicament you would be in, then, were I to accept the offer. I am half tempted to do so, out of pure spite. What right had you to be so certain I should not ? "

" How charmingly you exercise your feminine privilege ! The inconsistency of your question is delicious; but I am glad you ask it. I had no right, but several reasons, some which you would probably supply yourself; others, less obvious, from which you might dissent. First, because he stands in the way," and John pointed to the miniature which had not escaped his sharp eyes. " A very serious obstacle. To avoid all sentiment, I will simply say that a fish on the bank is worth a dozen in the brook, and besides, the captured one is magnificent. Secondly, because you still retain a suicidal independence of character. You might have chosen a beggar—you certainly have not, but that is beside the question—but you would not suffer an Emperor to be forced down your throat. And now we arrive at less obvious reasons. Because, in spite of your natural strength of will, you cannot now resist yourself; you have become your own slave, the most ignominious form of bondage."

"Thank you," interposed Theodora, with forced levity. "You are a charming advocate! What lady could resist your pleading? I must be grateful that at least you acknowledge my independence."

"And even that," said John, "has degenerated into mere capriciousness. It has ceased to be a redeeming quality. It is no longer a power, but a weakness. It is self-assertion, tending always to self-destruction; impotent to act save in one direction—downwards, always downwards. You may flutter and vacillate from this caprice to that and call it independence, but you must still follow your millstone—downwards. You pretend that yours is an imperial progress in vice, that your supremacy is optional; you glory in it, but you say to yourself, 'I reserve the right of abdication.' You believe that the voice which you ever hear urging you onward, bidding you trample down all remorse and scruple, bidding you revenge your wrongs on society by becoming its detestable delight, is the voice of your sovereign will, majestic even in infamy. It is all false; you cannot draw back if you would. If the vulture can suddenly abstain from carrion, or the swine take to delicate feeding, then can you halt and say, 'I will go no further.' Your will is deposed, its murmurs are drowned in hideous clamour; that which you listen to is the howl of rabid inclination, insatiable and uncontrollable. Your career is no longer a despotism of purpose, it is an anarchy of passion; its end will be a reign of terror, misery, and death!"

Again, from his lips as from Lupicina's, the awful warning which was beginning to terrify her—death! hell and death! misery and death! Were her nerve and her courage really failing her? No, of that she felt certain; she could face any material danger as undauntedly as ever. But this phantasmal horror, this shadowy abyss which every one saw gaping before her, there was something which appalled even her in that. She held this man in small account, but his merciless words, why did they stab her like repeated dagger blows? Were they true? She remembered that when she was beseeching Ecebolus to keep clear of her, her chief warning had been grounded on this same idea of self-perdition, that his weaker nature—for such she chose to believe it—would be extinguished in hers, even as it now seemed possible that the Theodora whom she had known and relied on might be merged in a creature of habitual vicious impulse, automatically vile, impotently in excess. She used to exult in her splendid, resolute iniquity, but the very essence of a resolution was in the power of changing it. Had she indeed lost this? What did this audacious adventurer mean by attacking her in this savage way, declaiming in that terrible sonorous monotone? Was he, too, among the prophets?

And once more she raised her beautiful face, pale with novel emotion, and struggled into indignant speech. "If all that men say be true, John of Cappadocia is hardly qualified to offer either warning or advice, even to such as I am."

John shook his head with an almost benignant smile. "It matters little whose lips utter the counsel if you acknowledge its truth and value, as in your heart you do. Whatever men may say of John of Cappadocia, no one can accuse him of letting his weaknesses interfere with his interests. But it is wasting time to vindicate myself. I do not preach against morality; I bid you beware of a complete collapse of all that is, or was, yourself. I would rather see in you ten times greater determination to evil than a pitiful self-abandonment. There is a vast difference between them; in the one the individuality is still vigorous, in the other it is paralyzed; in the one case there is at least a chance of a reaction, of a struggle and a triumph, in the other there is no hope—the end, the miserable end, is only a question of time. Theodora, listen. You hold your destiny in your hand. I believe that on no human being, man or woman, did fate ever bestow a more glorious opportunity; I wish I could believe that you will not reject it. I have carefully considered at what cost alone you can accept it now and renounce all else, and I dread your not being equal to the sacrifice. I fear that you have gone too far, and yet, perhaps, not far enough ; that you must sink lower before you can rise. The decree of Fate is unalterable, but your weak wilfulness may postpone its fulfilment. In the black depth of the abyss the knowledge that It has passed so near will save you from yourself and despair. Read the letter."

His last words were a gleam of light to Theodora. " My destiny ! " she exclaimed, in bitter scorn. " I see it all now; the grand future of my father's house, which has at last descended on me—at last ! The prophet himself has become the messenger of the gods ; " and with a harsh, nervous laugh she tore the letter open.

The Cappadocian leant back and watched her closely, not dissatisfied with himself and his diplomacy. From a desire to strengthen his young connection with Justinian and renew his old acquaintance with Theodora, he had undertaken a mission which from the first appeared to him quite hopeless. His belief in his own prophecies was thoroughly re-awakened by this time, but superstition in him did not preclude the exercise of that practical good sense, by which he saw the absurdity of expecting that Theodora would stop in mid-career and give up all which—— But we shall presently see what the letter required of her. His success had been far greater than he anticipated. He had succeeded in rousing and exciting her, in changing her vein of scornful indifference into strong, indignant interest, in partially humiliating and even terrifying her, by a fierce assault upon the point where she was most vulnerable. If once the idea could be forced upon her that she was no longer the relentless despot of her own passions, but their helpless victim, incapable of making an effort to escape, then there was a slight hope that the letter might be effectual—"and a very slight one it is," thought John, eyeing the miniature. Ah, if Crœso-Adonis could only be got rid of!

This is the letter which Theodora was reading :—

Justinian to Theodora.

"That I write this letter is at once the great shame and satisfaction of my life. The shame is the offspring of education, prejudice, and habitual reserve. The satisfaction is born of the consciousness that through no unbecoming caprice, through no sudden wantonness of inclination, but by earnest thought and laborious self-search, I have schooled myself into overcoming these obstacles, and am able to address you freely and without embarrassment.

"I would it were possible to ignore for the moment all considerations of personality and sex, and let my soul speak to yours. But above all things I desire to be practical. My life hitherto has been more prolific of theories than of aught else. And now, if my design appear somewhat visionary and fantastic, I am the more anxious to avoid any strain or ambiguity in the expression and execution of it.

"I first saw you at the Cynegium. The germ of which this letter is the fruit has not been too hastily matured. Through what subtle governing agency that germ was implanted in a soil apparently so uncongenial as my breast, I have long ceased to inquire. Enough that it was so implanted, and from that time to this its development has been steady and continuous.

"By that earliest impression of you I gauge my present feelings. It was a spiritual, not a carnal impulse, far more intense and enduring than the material emotions which spring simply from the contemplation of perfect loveliness. I have since seen you at the theatre, so that these last words are not without meaning.

"There are present to my mind two Theodoras, and on either image I can dwell with delight. They are counterparts, twain and yet one, distinct and yet identical. The one is the sequel and consummation of the other. Neither belongs to the present; the one is a past reality, the other a dream of the future.

"The one is the young suppliant of the Cynegium,

showing, in her pure maiden beauty, like some exquisite opening blossom—pale, fragile, in peril and distress, undergoing insult and humiliation, but through all triumphantly upheld by the indomitable constancy of the soul within.

"The other is also the heroine of a triumph, of a far greater one. The peril through which she has passed is more fearful, the insult and humiliation which she has undergone are a thousand times more terrible, for they were self-inflicted upon her own fair body and soul. But she too has triumphed. I see her purified and repentant, striving patiently to efface by a noble womanhood the hideous memories of her youth. And before these two visions I, Justinian, bow myself with reverent love.

"But they stand far apart. And between them a third rises, resembling both so far as it possesses their common attribute of beauty, but no further. And at the sight of it man shudders, devils exult, and angels weep. In my madness I have dared to gaze on this also, and if God be merciful to me, I will never look upon it again, lest my heart and brain be withered.

"Must this dark presence wax in horror until it absorb and eclipse to all eternity the fair visions on either hand, or shall it sink back into the abyss which gave it birth, leaving them free to blend into one perfect whole ?

"The answer rests with you. By what shall I

adjure you? What words can I find strong enough
to express the intensity of appeal that is in me?
My soul lies prostrate before yours, supplicating it
to have mercy on both. Do not stop your ears
against its cry. My heart weeps and bleeds in its
agony of entreaty; let its tears and blood touch
yours. But one effort is needed, one noble effort,
worthy of what you were, worthy of what you may
yet be. Be strong, and I will help you. If I could
not rescue you in the Cynegium, I can do so now.
Cast off the devil's bonds which bind you to an
accursed calling and a hateful life, to a slavery
more dreadful than the most dreadful death. Cast
them off and be free. I will provide for you a
refuge where you will be safe and unmolested, and
tenderly cared for; a sanctuary from the world,
from your present self, and—from me; where all
your surroundings shall inspire peacefulness and
hope; where, not by harsh penance and dreary
discipline, but by tranquil reflection and cheerful
well-doing, you shall learn to attune your purified
spirit to nobler ends; to look back without despair,
and to look forward without presumption.

"For the rest I am content to trust to the future.
I make no bargain and require no promise; my
offer is unconditional. Only let me save you now;
let me answer the appeal which your soul once
made to mine, and redeem the gift of God from the
hellish hands into which it has fallen.

"If, in answer to my prayer, you will attempt and achieve this self-conquest and self-deliverance, then I swear that whatever future God may have in store for me, a share in that future shall be yours, if you choose to claim it; whatever befall me, I will acknowledge the claim with gratitude and love. The barriers which the tyrannical decree of man raises between us shall then cease to exist for me; their insignificant fabric shall vanish before the breath of a solemn resolve like mine; and in saying this I am not unconscious that the time may come when he who criticizes an act of Justinian's must answer for it to the lord of the East.

"To write thus is no trivial proof how far I believe and trust in your nobler nature. By that nature and your dauntless heart which shall triumph, by your soul which shall be rescued from perdition, by your fair body which shall be purified, by your beauty which shall be sanctified and worshipped, by the memory of your father's wrongs and your own which shall be redressed, I implore you not to reject this offer. The greater the difficulty the greater will be the victory, and the more clearly you will vindicate my choice.

"If ever your heart feel faint and your task seem greater than you can perform, look on that sapphire, and remember that when you have won the fight, he who takes it for his token is ready to fulfil to the letter all that is written here.

" Within three days I shall expect your answer. If you consent, I will ask for one interview, and then, not until you return me the bracelet with the message, 'I have conquered,' will I see you again. May God be merciful to us both ! "

CHAPTER VIII.

SAPPHIRE OR EMERALD ?

"WILL you wait and take back my answer?" said Theodora quietly, when she had finished reading. "I will not detain you long." But John saw that her composure was forced. Her voice was hard and strained, and she was very pale.

"You are determined to refuse?" he said. "For Heaven's sake, do not decide hastily. I know the difficulties of the situation, but at least give yourself time to reflect. Think of all that letter means——"

She stopped his remonstrances. "It is useless to argue with me. But I was mistaken about you. I ask your pardon, and thank you most sincerely. Will you wait here?"

"I intend to call on Chrysomalla to-day," said John. "I will pay my visit now, and return in an hour. Do not write your answer before then, at least. Theodora, my brave girl, let me entreat you——"

" Stop ! " exclaimed Theodora, harshly. " I have no choice. I must—I must refuse ! Go now, and return in the hour."

John looked at her set white face and furrowed brow, and left the room.

" Must, must ! " he muttered to himself; " what is at the back of that ' must ' ? Whatever it may be it turns the scale against Justinian. I never thought to bring her so near accepting." And gathering a crumb of satisfaction from this reflection he entered Chrysomalla's apartments.

But Theodora, left to herself, sank into a chair with her mind in a whirl of turbulent emotion, from which for a time it was hard to single out for consideration any particular idea. Her dominant perceptions were utter amazement, gratified vanity, and a stinging sense of pain, which, if not actually bitter discontent and regret, was closely akin to both.

" At the Cynegium," she thought. " So long, long ago ! Surely centuries have passed since then, since I was a pure, innocent maiden ! And he can write such a letter as this to me now ! In all the city this paragon can find no woman to suit him but Theodora ! What am I ? Am I a devil in angel's form, or an angel doing penance in the shape of a devil ? There are beautiful devils as well as hideous ones. If I could only see and understand myself ! Had I not sworn by the memory of my father, how should I act now? Should I accept or refuse? The Cappadocian was right; no one in the world has ever had an opportunity like this. What fresh piece of monstrous folly and wickedness am I about to commit? It seems to me as if, having heaven and earth in my grasp, I am going to cast them away like a broken bracelet. How tenderly and mercifully he writes of me, and with what proud confidence in himself; not the shadow of a doubt as to his own future, And he offers that future to me! His imperial mind can humble itself in supplication before my guilty soul. And this is the man I have sworn to horrify and disgust!" She covered her face for a moment with her hands, and then sprang up, crying aloud, "I dare not think any longer; it must be done. I will make short work of it;" and hurried into the other room—to find Ecebolus waiting for her, lounging magnificently on a sofa and playing with her lapdog.

For the first time the sight of his beautiful face caused her a thrill of annoyance.

"You here!" she exclaimed, and her tone was not one of pleased surprise.

"Why that emphatic 'you'?" said the young Tyrian, rising; "is my presence here so remarkable? I flattered myself I was expected, and should be welcome."

"Well, on the whole, perhaps you are," said The̶ ̶ ̶ ̶ ̶ ̶ ̶ ̶ ̶ ̶ ̶ ̶ ̶ ̶

"What is the matter?" said Ecebolus caress-
ingly, as he took hold of her hands and drew her
towards him; "you look pale and distressed.
Something has gone wrong."

"I am not well to-day," she answered, avoiding
his dark, searching eyes. "My head aches,
and—— " she hesitated for an instant.

"And you have a slight cold, an attack of the
nerves, and feel feverish," interposed Ecebolus,
smiling. "Is that it? No, no, this kind of excuse
will not serve you; little indispositions are not
the least in your line. One of your greatest
charms in my eyes is your unexceptionably perfect health. I dislike delicate people, especially
women."

"Then you had better take a stroll to the Porta
Piscaria and admire the fish-wives; you will find
them as robust as you can desire."

"The hint is lost upon me. Come, let me try
if I can't surprise you out of your headache. Do
you remember once longing for something which
you thought it impossible to get?"

"What a very vague question!" exclaimed
Theodora pettishly, "considering how many things
I have longed for in my time."

"I hope not often in vain," said Ecebolus,
"since I have had the happiness of studying your
wishes. At all events, I have brought the something I mean with me, and here it is." He took

up a box which lay on the sofa, a few inches long, and delicately carved in perfumed wood; and opening it, drew out a thin roll, which, by dint of sundry careful shakings and unfoldings, developed itself into a loose robe of average dimensions, but of a texture so marvellously fine and diaphonous, that as Ecebolus held it at arm's length it looked more like a floating film of pearly vapour than a material garment. "There," said the Tyrian, in a tone of triumph, and gently agitating the gossamer folds; "there it is at last; a robe of sea-silk, the real textile zephyr. I have had greater trouble in securing this than I ever had over anything in my life, except yourself. As far as I can discover, only three have ever been made."

Taking rarity and the fancy of the day as a standard of value, it was a splendid gift, worthy of an Empress, and had cost more gold pieces than Ecebolus cared to recollect; a robe woven of the silky filaments by which the pinna, a species of bivalve shell, is attached to the rocks. But Theodora was in no humour to appreciate it. One of what Chrysomalla used to call "her Cornelia fits" was upon her. The offering was ill-timed. Its costly triviality and even its sensual suggestiveness were for the moment intensely distasteful to her, by contrast with the solid assurances of the sapphire bracelet. She thought, with bitter scorn, how differently these two men wooed; how intrinsically inferior was the ostentatious suit of Ecebolus to that of his rival. In another mood she might have made the very same comparison all in favour of the ardent, practical Tyrian. No woman was ever more "uncertain and hard to please" than Theodora. I omit the third epithet as scarcely applicable. Had Ecebolus been a wise man he would have deferred the production of his prize until that look of pain and discontent had left his lady-love's face.

She merely glanced at the precious tissue, and said coldly, "Thank you. It seems pretty, what there is of it, and is, no doubt, very valuable. I will take your word for that. You ought to be a good judge of silk."

Ecebolus coloured, but answered off-hand, with a short laugh. "I am; I had some real experience in the trade once. But the robe ceases to be valuable when it affords you no pleasure." And he tossed it carelessly on to the couch.

Then Theodora turned to him, and, resting her small hands on his shoulders, looked up into his splendid eyes until the vexation died out of them.

"Ecebolus," she said, "forgive me. I cannot behave well to-day. I am troubled about something."

"My sweet girl, I know it," said the young man

smoothing back her chestnut locks. "I knew it directly I set eyes upon you. You have such a tell-tale brow." And he stooped to kiss the brow in question.

She went on. "Ecebolus, will you not think better of it, and give me up before it is too late? Marry some girl worthy of you—you have only to choose—and let her have the house and everything else, and leave me to go my own way. Remember what I once said to you—I shall be your ruin."

"Nonsense, child!" he answered. "I thought we had agreed to forget all that. As for that trumpery gauze, it is nothing. Wait until the races; and when the team has won you shall have a present in earnest. I can hardly reckon how much I stand in." He could not get his gold pieces out of his head.

"And if the team does not win?" asked Theodora.

But Ecebolus laid his hand upon her upturned mouth. "Words of ill omen!" he exclaimed, with all the superstition of a gambler. "How could you say that? Not win! Ask Demas. He declares the Blues won't be round the last goal before we breast the cord."

"May I see your horses?"

"To be sure you may, if you will promise not to make any unlucky speeches about losing and ruin.

I will take you up to the training ground to see
them gallop."

"I will be very careful," said Theodora, meekly.
"But, ah me!" she replied, "you will not understand. We don't mean quite the same thing by
ruin."

"I know, I know," said Ecebolus, again closing
her lips, this time in another fashion. "Let it pass.
And now tell me what is troubling you. What
is that letter in your hand?"

"A love-letter. Don't be vexed. You know I
get so many of them. I can't help it. But this
one—— "

"But this one?" repeated Ecebolus, bravely
gulping down a disagreeable sensation.

"This one is rather different to the rest. It
must be answered."

"And supposing it must be? I don't see the
necessity; but what then? Who is the writer?"

"Don't ask me. I cannot tell you, or show you
the letter."

"Of course I don't care about seeing fellows'
letters," said Ecebolus; "but what does the fool
want?"

"He offers me a great deal."

"More than I do?"

"Well, as much, I suppose; himself and—
everything he can."

"Hem! And perhaps it annoys you to refuse?"

" No, it is not that. I am vexed at the manner in which I am obliged to refuse."

" Upon my soul, I don't understand. Do speak plainly."

" This man makes me a very noble offer—I cannot explain how noble ; and I must send him the most detestable answer I can think of."

" And why the—why on earth must you do that ? "

" To make him hate and despise me, and never think of me any more for ever except with disgust."

" This is unpleasantly mysterious. I don't object, naturally ; but for the life of me I cannot see why you don't send a civil but decided ' No.' Poor devil ! "

" And that I cannot explain either. I only tell you what I am forced to do, and that ought to content you."

" What a pertinacious beggar it must be ! Is he good-looking—better-looking than I am ? "

" Absurd ! You know well that no one is half as handsome as you are. No, I should call him rather plain, and he is getting bald."

" Then, depend upon it, he is touchy on that point. Tell him to look in the mirror, and send him that miniature ; and if he wants more refer him to the original. I'll undertake to disgust him."

Ecebolus spoke in jest, but she caught at the notion. It was capable, she thought, of development.

"Do you know, that is not a bad idea of yours," she said.

"I am rather celebrated for making happy suggestions in cases of emergency. But I wish I could understand why there should be such a fuss over this hideous stranger."

"I never said he was hideous. Some day, perhaps, you shall know all; that will depend upon your behaviour."

"Thank you," said Ecebolus, with ironical courtesy; "it shall be my earnest endeavour to deserve such implicit confidence. Now you had better get your disgusting letter off your mind, and be sure you enclose this with my message." And he handed her the miniature, which he had been taking out of its setting.

"No," she said, "it is a pity. It is so like, and exquisitely painted."

"Pshaw! What matters the picture when you possess the reality? But what is that you have got besides the letter?"

"A bracelet."

"Blue, by Jove!" exclaimed Ecebolus, examining the stone. "The fellow, whoever he is, is my natural enemy. I should like to have a bet with him. Emerald against sapphire for all I am worth."

Theodora was gazing at the portrait. At the Tyrian's words she looked up with a sudden terror in her face.

"Yes," she exclaimed, "he will be your enemy, and all through me! I will not send this; put it back. Let him hate me only. He is powerful, and will never forgive you."

"Forgive me!" cried Ecebolus, in utter scorn and amazement. "Now, this is too much. I will find out the name of this bald-headed bugbear, if I have to follow your messenger."

"No, no, you will not do that!" said Theodora, clinging to his arm.

"Not if you promise to send the miniature. I was only joking to begin with, but you have made it a point of honour with me. Do you suppose I am afraid of him, whoever he is? It shall go."

"Ecebolus, I know you are not afraid of anybody or anything, but it would be in such bad taste."

"I can afford to indulge in bad taste if I like. It either goes, or I do in person."

"After all, is there any better way?" she thought. "And you will not try to find out who it is?"

"Not if you send it. I don't care about playing spy; I do hope that this sort of thing is exceptional. For once it is not uninteresting, but it might pall upon one after a time."

"Remember our bargain," said Theodora, turning upon him sharply; but she added in a softer voice, "You need not be afraid, Ecebolus; it will never happen again."

In a few minutes she wrote her letter :—

"I thank you for your offer. You are quite mistaken about me. I am simply a woman, and follow female instincts, especially those of my class. If it be a question of choice between two men, judge for yourself whether I am likely to hesitate. I thank you for returning my old bracelet. The new stone is handsome, and worth a good sum.—THEODORA."

Then she made up a packet with the miniature, and something else which she went into another room to fetch; and lastly, selecting a silver casket from amongst the many costly knick-knacks before her, she placed in it Justinian's letter, and set fire to the paper, watching it until it was quite consumed, with set lips and a steadfast frown.

Ecebolus regarded all these proceedings with uneasy curiosity. He was perplexed and annoyed by Theodora's extreme seriousness and severe face. At last he cried, "Are you actually going to keep the ashes of the fellow's letter ?"

She looked at him with a strange smile.

"They are the ashes of my life and soul, which I have sacrificed as a burnt-offering to you, O Apollo!"

"Well, it beats me," said Ecebolus, in a tone of despair. "Have you given my message?"

"Certainly not. You would not really care to swagger like a Faction bully?"

"Have you told him to look in the mirror?"

"I have done more; I have sent him the mirror to look in."

"No!" exclaimed Ecebolus, with almost boyish enjoyment. "What a joke it is! How savage the old satyr will be!"

The handsome Tyrian was not without good points, in spite of his fashionable profligacy. He was gallant and generous, and not vicious at heart. But, as I forewarned my readers, he was no hero. As Demas might have said, there was a suspicion of hair about his heels.

An hour afterwards, Justinian was sitting quite still and silent, with Theodora's letter crushed in his clenched hand. John the Cappadocian, who also sat by and watched him, thought that he had never before seen human face express such terrific intensity of murderous wrath; the more terrific that it found no vent in sound. At length, however, Justinian parted his dry, livid lips and broke the silence.

"I claim my right. What was the one act of your life which you hesitated to confess?"

"I was the chief agent in the abduction of the Patriarch Macedonius."

"It was a detestable deed!" cried Justinian, in a loud, fierce tone, as if he challenged contradiction.

"It was a necessary one," replied John, with perfect calmness. "The question was simple; sovereign or subject, which was to be master? It became imperative that his Holiness should be removed. Some one had to be found who would dare to do it. Whether the sentence on the criminal be just or unjust it must be carried out."

"But all men hate the executioner."

"And fear him," said John. "If the time should ever come, sir, for you to realize how the obstinate interference of one man may thwart your most cherished schemes, you may also realize that the sword of justice is a more admirable adjunct than her scales."

And Justinian allowed this brazen speech to pass unnoticed.

After a pause, the Cappadocian recommenced.

"Whilst waiting for that letter, I took the opportunity of making certain inquiries. The Lady Lupicina was with Theodora last night."

A lightning gleam flashed over Justinian's brooding countenance.

"Then this cruel answer may have been written at her instigation!"

"I think there can be little doubt on that point," said John.

"It must be so. It is impossible I could have been so completely mistaken in any one." The real wound, after all, had been inflicted on Justinian's self-esteem. "How much has Theodora told him?" he added, indicating the miniature.

"Little or nothing," said John, confidently. "At your next meeting with him you will be able to decide."

Justinian rose and carefully locked away in a cabinet the miniature, the small jewelled hand-mirror which Theodora had sent, and her letter.

"She has kept the bracelet," he muttered. "I will not judge too hastily."

Then he turned again to the Cappadocian.

"My good friend and counsellor, advise me. I have been much disturbed lately; I require distraction and amusement. What shall I do?"

"You anticipate my intention, sir," said John, whose usually steady-going heart throbbed with a sense of victory. "I was on the point of hazarding a proposal. Become the champion of the Blue Faction at the next races. The Greens look forward to an easy triumph. There are no horses in Constantinople equal to the team of Ecebolus,

except those of the Imperial breed now in your
uncle's stables. They are superior. Put them into
the trainer's hands at once. If the Tyrian does
not win, all his silk-looms will hardly save him
from ruin. Try the Hippodrome; I venture to
think that you will find this novel pursuit not
without interest, and you will acquire an immense
amount of valuable popularity."

END OF VOL. II.

www.ingramcontent.com/pod-product-compliance
Lightning Source LLC
Chambersburg PA
CBHW020848020726
47497CB00005B/1306